CROSS WINDS

Other Books by Edward Allen Karr

SERIES: Socrates Lewis Stories
(Psychological/Religious Fiction)

Crossovers – Book Two

* * * * *

SERIES: Fringes Of Infinity
(Contemporary Fantasy Fiction)

Lin Finity and her Mayhem Rising – Book One
Lin Finity in Holding On – A Novella
Lin Finity and the Words Unspoken – Book Two
Lin Finity and the Islands of Time – Book Three
Lin Finity and the Flights to Forever – Book Four
Tayo Tersoo and the Hunter of Souls – Book Five

* * * * *

SERIES: Thrills N Kills in The Hills
(Racy, Comical Horror in Beverly Hills)

Dayzee Dazzle and the Kildare Killers – Book One
Dayzee Dazzle and her Manic Mansion – Book Two
Dayzee Dazzle and the On-Set Onslaught – Book Three
Dayzee Dazzle and the Cadaver Collectors – Book Four

* * * * *

SERIES: A World So Close
(Middle-grade Fantasy Adventure & Coming of Age)

Jayden Blue and the Gift to Imagine – A Prequel
Jayden Blue and the Sword in his Shadow – Book One
Jayden Blue and the Call of the Wings – Book Two
Jayden Blue and the Lair of the Iron Lions – Book Three
Jayden Blue and the Journey to Val ka'Yoom – Book Four
Jayden Blue and the Forest of Night Fallen – Book Five
Jayden Blue and the Wait of the Sun – Book Six

* * * * *

CROSS WINDS

Socrates Lewis Stories Book One

Edward Allen Karr

LAKESIDE LETTERS, LLC

Lakeside Letters, LLC
30628 Detroit Road, #247
Westlake, OH 44145

This is a work of fiction. Names, characters, businesses, events, and incidents are the products of the author's imagination. Any resemblance to actual persons, living or dead, or actual events is purely coincidental. Certain long-standing institutions are mentioned, but the characters are imaginary. The opinions expressed are those of the characters and should not be confused with those of the author.

First Edition, 2024
Lakeside Letters, LLC

Cover design by JD Smith Design

ISBN-13: 978-1-950886-60-9

Author's Note

"I'm not publishing this," she said as she handed me the unsealed envelope. "For a variety of reasons, I'd prefer that you do it."

Mara (not her real name) and I held our first meeting on a frozen, snow-crusted bench in Central Park in early December. An unexpectedly falling temperature and merciless snowfall prompted us to sit close, as if we already knew each other well.

Before I could ask, "Why me?" she explained that she'd been following my novels and felt that if I were to present the material in a more story-like format, she'd likely be spared any questions or commentary regarding any of the ideas in the manuscript.

I remember staring at her after that comment, then opening what she'd handed me while telling her that I'd gladly consider writing the thing up as fiction, then—I really had no certainty that any part of the story was factual anyway.

My method is to scrutinize first the beginning, then the end. It's the way my stories are concocted too: beginning, end, fill it all in. I saw the title, "Crosswinds," then flipped through the manuscript, noting that it was the original and mechanically typed, complete with a few smudges.

At the very end, handwritten, was the name Socrates Lewis and a date about two months prior.

I know now that the small stain in the lower left corner near his name is from a whiskey spill, which brand I couldn't tell you.

Mara had been watching me scan through it, saw that I'd gotten to the author's name, then said, "That's not his real first name. He fancies himself to be some kind of philosopher."

I only nodded as I began reading from the beginning. She let me peruse the entirety of it without interruption, but her stare on the left side of my face felt like it delivered some needed warmth as heavy snowflakes fell all around us.

After I'd finished reading, I turned to Mara, who obviously had been scrutinizing my reaction to it, and explained my own philosophy on writing. And that is that painters paint with colors of their choosing. In a similar way, writers paint with ideas. I told her that I couldn't imagine anyone berating a painter for using any particular color, and readers, I assured her, are of the same mindset: a book can and should be painted with any ideas that tell a story worth reading.

She didn't seem entirely convinced, but I did accept this magazine editor's request and wrote up the Socrates piece in a fiction format, leaving his title in place. Mara read my draft and suggested that we meet again. It had been another two months or so, and I wondered if she'd somehow found more of Socrates's notes.

Knowing each other better this time, and subjecting ourselves to worse weather than at that first meet, we again sat close. I expected her to hand me more of Socrates's writings or perhaps some of her own notes, but she only wanted to talk.

Apparently, I'd captured the essence of his tale with sufficient depth and exactitude. My embellishments, she said, were scarce enough and probably imbued it with more sense of normalcy than what actually had transpired.

She was also amused by my characterization of her and assured me that she's not at all so difficult. Thankfully, my apology was accepted.

She said that she'd considered hiring an investigator to look into the existence of Miley and if she was real, whether anything in her life matched Socrates's narrative of her. But her conclusion was that not having any proof that any of his writing was factual might be the most prudent course.

With a smile, in defiance of the cold wind, Mara said that she'd met with Socrates just a few days earlier. Her smile was because she told me of him wearing a shoestring around his neck with something very special still knotted to it. He'd told her that he planned to soon try to place it where he'd always thought it truly belonged.

Of course, I couldn't even organize my questions quickly enough, and she continued, her smile gone and a frown developing, probably from the cold, as she gazed at me from so near.

She said that she'd shown Socrates's work to only one other person, she wouldn't disclose whom. That individual lingered with some fascination on the final words written by Socrates, a statement about belief. This person then concluded that Socrates was the right person to chase down a curious story recently presented to her in a casual way and without further details.

Socrates, Mara said, agreed to look into it and if there's a worthwhile story there, he'd record it all in another manuscript. Again, with his typewriter, I'd guess.

And the plan is for me to take his next manuscript and polish it up for publication as a sequel of sorts.

I don't yet know the title.

I'll leave that to the writer, self-proclaimed philosopher, and whiskey devotee, Socrates Lewis.

~ Edward Allen Karr

Excerpt

From Chapter 3 – Unless You're Already a Madman

She shook her head and said, "Really, nobody sent you?"

"Huh?"

She grinned at his confused look, then focused again on the scissors, only the two points visible in the murky puddle.

"I'm Miley. You seem nice. You should probably just stay the hell away from me."

Without waiting for a response, she turned and began to give herself to the mist and gloom, and Socrates just watched her walking away.

Before he'd lost sight of her completely, she turned just enough to see him.

"Unless you're already a madman," she said.

Table of Contents

Chapter 1 – That Damn Wind

"Jesus, I really have to quit talking to myself."

Socrates Lewis studied the tired eyes gazing back at him, the pair of them taking turns on one side of the shoestring, then the other. The pupils seemed to have become snared in webs of fine, jagged red lines.

Eyes still locked, he guided his left hand up, aimed it well, and pinched the string right between his reflected eyes, stopping its accidental play as a pendulum above his dresser, where it hung from three neat layers of tape clinging to the mirror's top frame.

Focused too intently to blink, he held it still.

Then backed his hand away.

"Dammit."

He'd returned his left arm to his side, matching his right, and he saw undeniable proof that he was leaning to his left.

A quick glance to the string's bottom end confirmed that it was hanging plumb.

The ring at its end, though, revolved casually, changing directions after it had twisted the string as far as it could, oblivious to its contribution in revealing his malady in such a simple, unarguable way.

He'd just begun to let his lungs leak out what they'd held inside so as to not corrupt his exam, when the alarm clock on his nightstand began a steady, troublesome buzzing.

"Jesus."

A few quick steps to his right got him close enough to wrestle it around with his right hand, its protests unrelenting until he'd found the button.

He shut off the offensive device with an impatient click.

Leaving his hand on it, like pinning down a small beast to enforce some measure of quiet from it, he turned his eyes to the worn hardcover book lying next to it.

A study of the wit and wisdom of one Socrates.

The philosopher.

The real one.

The source for Socrates Lewis's adopted first name.

He set free the clock beast to rest four fingertips on the book, then drummed them all in sequence several times.

His fingers got quiet when he looked up at the small open window right above the nightstand's dim lamp, which struggled to light the surface below it and left the rest of the room to its gloom.

The dingy gray walls close all around him.

A ceiling dark and hanging low above him.

His view through the wet screen couldn't reach far—only across an alley to the weathered gray bricks of a multi-story structure much like what housed Socrates's home. Most windows there were dark, but some gave signs that life stirred, maybe not welcoming the drizzly Monday morning but complying all the same.

He felt the wind.

It carried the ripe scents of whatever the rain had splashed around on the alley pavement two stories below.

On the way back to his mirror, he fought to arrange his face to show indifference, an acceptance, even, of what he might see.

But his face grimaced back at him, both eyes staring out from the left side of his indicator string.

He turned his head toward the open window, and he looked into the oncoming light traces of wind, no longer able to disguise his disgust by imposing calm on his face.

"That damn wind."

He stepped back over to the window and slammed it shut.

Again, he checked the degree of his affliction.

He found that his right eye had crept closer to the string.

"That's good. That helps."

Looking down toward the right, between piles of jumbled clothes, an aged fedora, a paper plate with remains of lunch from two days past, and streaks of birdseed that had evaded sweeps to gather it up, a half-full bottle of whiskey looked back.

Waiting patiently.

With its close compatriot, a smudged and stained clear glass tumbler.

A hand found each of them.

One poured from the bottle, while the other held the glass still.

Before taking a leisurely swig and swallow, he held the glass near his right cheek and stared at the man looking back at him.

He again checked his degree of plumb.

It was still off.

But not as much as before.

He allowed himself a quick sip, then held the glass partway to his right, never losing sight of his leaning companion.

Who leaned slightly less.

A grin lodged itself in a face that had needed a shave three days earlier. The grin grew as he extended his hand, and the glass, all the way to the right.

The grin became an actual smile, and he offered some satisfied nodding to the upright image, which he saw was bisected neatly by a calm string weighted down by a ring with a single sparkling jewel and tracing a direct path down between the eyes.

He chuckled softly and said, "Huh. I do know this: whiskey can balance things out."

With his eyes focused on the approaching glass, seeing that it had more to offer than serving as a makeshift counterbalance, he brought it near and downed the last of it.

While reluctantly turning his eyes back to his other eyes, he found a spot on his dresser for the empty glass, grinding and scattering seeds.

Both eyes, still sending out thin red filaments to mar the white regions, mocked him from the left side of his handy string.

He winced at the sight.

"Tragically, using whiskey that way lacks permanence."

He fumbled around until he'd snagged the neck of the bottle.

Then, he gave himself an accepting grin.

"Always will."

He groped and rummaged around on the dresser top before allowing his eyes to assist, and he grabbed at the closest pile with his free hand. But he only gripped the top item briefly as he studied the unfolded sweatshirt, then he let it go and raised his hand high enough to lose contact.

Then, he patted every pile he could reach and pulled his hand away.

"That'll just have to be okay. Just . . . like that."

A moment later, he snatched up the nearest crumpled dress shirt, half-buried in a mound off to the right.

A quick snap of it with one hand shook loose some seed. He then let go of the bottle to get started dressing himself.

*   *   *

He kept his well-worn shoes in contact with the tile floor of his kitchen as he ambled toward the refrigerator. An abrupt stop midway, then two steps backwards allowed him to flip on the overhead light. Two of the four bare bulbs responded, casting a shroud of light over the small table with two chairs near it in the middle of the room.

Before continuing to scrounge for a snack before breakfast, he stared down at the typewriter busy collecting dust. A blank sheet had been installed, he couldn't remember exactly how long before, and he winced at it as it seemed to goad him, compelling him to acknowledge its yearning for words. Even a letter or two.

He saw that the paper had collected some dust too.

He leaned toward it, gave it a snap with a finger, and scoffed at the cloud of fine particles that he'd scattered up and around.

"Soon."

Straightening and spinning slightly put him again within grabbing distance of the fridge handle, which he gave a modest pull.

It held its ground, so he tried again, and it protested with a weak, protracted whine as its muted interior light barely scratched the drabness of the room.

After retrieving a slice of pizza, which was mostly crust, from a paper plate in there, he took a bite and leaned backwards to shut the door.

He'd just started chewing when his cell phone, somewhere on the table, began buzzing and vibrating, demanding that he postpone the next bite.

While chomping off another chewy portion anyway, he held the phone up and saw that it was Mara interrupting his snack. He lowered the phone to his side, shook his head, then reached out to drop it back where he'd found it.

But he didn't set it down. Instead, he tapped it with a finger from the hand holding the pizza, then held it to his ear.

"Hello, Mara. Jesus, Monday hasn't even slammed into us yet."

He sank teeth into crust while listening to her chirpy rant.

"I slammed into it first—we try to hit the ground running here. Deadlines are a real thing."

Mara, an attractive late-20s woman, was dressed too well to likely care about the content of the magazine she edited. She was half-sitting against a desk in a neat, organized office, a cell phone to her ear as she studied her stylish manicure.

After wedging most of the bite off to one side, Socrates sighed and answered her.

"Hell, that's probably right. So, tell me. What's my deadline?"

He held up his left hand, which had been emptied of the days-old leftovers, and studied his fingernails.

"Let's just say it's about to crash into you. Do another piece like that last one, which was damn good but freakin' ages ago."

He switched phone hands and gave the other nails an inspection.

"Maybe aim for something a bit more lighthearted this time."

"What the hell is lighthearted about life?" he said. "Nothing. Not when our minds aren't made to understand complex nuances of an existence that—"

"Stop. You're just not as deep as you like to believe. You're a lonely man in a shabby apartment, probably drinking your breakfast. Put the drink down. Write something."

He grinned at the glass he'd filled and left on the table, then picked it up.

"Hell, anyone can write 'something.' I don't know, but I think my life is more about—"

"Hold it. Here's just one of your problems: you insist on going by the name of someone who never wrote a damn thing. Do you even remember your real name anymore?"

He set the glass down quietly but didn't let it go.

"Jesus, Mara. Yeah. Of course. And I think I'm close to a deep insight into something major. Real soon, I'll—"

"Dump out your damn drink, Socrates, and get your ass to work. Maybe there is no deep meaning. Ever consider that?"

He paused to grin and swirled his whiskey around in a lazy wave, scraping a few stray seeds across the table.

"Are you the best choice to be running a mag on philosophy? Ever consider that?"

He leaned his head away from the phone and frowned from her snippy response.

"Write something. Something is better than nothing."

"Jesus. You—"

"Now."

He pulled the phone away, gave it a look, and saw that she'd ended the call. So, he set it down next to the bottle.

They were close, so he tapped his fingernails against the bottle, adding a brief staccato rhythm to the lifeless room.

"No, Mara. Whiskey is better than nothing."

He kept tapping with his right, then finished off the glass in his left. Before putting it down, he tipped it and peered inside. He scoffed.

"Or nothingness."

∗　∗　∗

Bottle in one hand, its neck clutched with no chance of escape, and a half-full glass in the other, also held tight as he used one finger to scratch around an eye, Socrates ventured back into the shadows of his bedroom.

Facing his mirror and its string, which had a calm and stationary ring knotted to its end, almost resting on bits of birdseed, he frowned at seeing a distinct lean to his left.

Appalled but captivated by the sight, he didn't stop studying it as he wedged into the dresser's messes first the glass on the left, then the bottle on the right.

Freed of the glass for the moment, his left hand cooperated and displayed in front of his face the lengths of all the nails. Before reaching any conclusion, he used the sharp one on the small finger of his right hand to pry a single seed out from its hideaway beneath a nail on the left hand.

It popped out and fell silently to the floor.

"I should let at least one pigeon in here, shouldn't I?"

He laughed and started biting at the nails on the left hand, not caring where they might land and stick as he spat them out. After a quick inspection, he dropped the arm straight to his side and checked the status.

"Huh. That helped."

He kept his hand at his side and only glanced down at it.

"They can't weigh much but maybe if I trimmed a little more, it would—"

He turned toward the window, which was still closed, then forgot the nails long enough to go to it and slide it back up, letting in more wind. He paused for only a moment to watch narrow rain rivers trace odd patterns along the glass.

"Rain. Lovely."

He positioned himself again to check his balance, his symmetry, and saw that he'd lost every nail-biting gain that he'd made.

"It's the wind," he said, frowning at the face in the mirror. "It's the goddamn wind. How the hell do I get fresh air and still stop the damn wind? Is there any goddamn person that knows? But my nails, those can always be—"

He jumped at the cell phone in his pocket singing out as it vibrated and bounced around. A quick glance at the caller ID led to a single tap and repositioning of it against his ear.

"Lynnie. How are you?"

"Fine, Dad. First, I have to ask: what's for breakfast over there?"

He took a second to look down at his glass but didn't pick it up.

"I'm about ready to hike down to the park, maybe see if that hot dog wagon guy is rolling through there yet."

Lynnie was dressed conservatively and in her early-20s. She sat at a small, neat table in a colorful, well-lit kitchen. A stack of textbooks and notebooks was near, and vapor spiraled up from a coffee mug.

"Carnival food again. Eh. Could be worse."

"Oh, yeah. Always. I'd be lost without that every day."

"Hey, mom still wants to hear from you. Give her a call, alright?"

He picked up his glass and frowned at the liquid as he spun it around.

"You know it's awkward, Hon. It's been too long since we've talked."

"Yep. Yeah, but call her anyway. I'm tired of hearing her complain about it."

He gestured with the glass toward the mirror as he answered, but his eyes were pointed somewhere above it.

"She never got past me switching majors to philosophy way back when. That's what started all the—"

"She caught you with a hooker, Dad. I would have nuked an engagement over behavior like that too."

The glass froze mid-gesture.

"Jesus, Lynnie. Yeah. That—"

"Again with Jesus? You really should show more respect."

The glass came down, almost striking the dresser and almost spilling.

"It's just a word, and I—"

Her sharp, single laugh silenced him.

"Sure. Just a word. Tell him that when you meet him."

"I, uh, I will. If we do meet."

"Anyway, she's right: you should have kept going with the accounting stuff."

"Probably. Yeah. Math didn't like me, though."

"I know. You never could balance even a checkbook. Still got that ring that you couldn't give away?"

He glared down at the ring on the string before downing the entire glass, but he set it down quietly and held the phone away to cough once.

"Yeah, it still has some value to me."

"Well, it's still a good ring, right?"

"Uh, yeah. Sure."

"How about that hat Mom gave you way back when? Still have that?"

"Of course. I'd never give that up, not even for a minute."

"Good. Had to check."

"You could see for yourself, Lynnie, if we could someday—"

"Uh, let's just be happy with our phone chats, alright?"

He took a moment to let a breath leak out quietly.

"Sure. Yeah, I do like our calls."

"Alright," she said, "hunt down that nutritious breakfast. See ya."

He gave the phone one last look, then sighed and set it down near the empty glass.

"Kids. Editors too."

He re-established a solid hold on the bottle's neck and shook his head while watching the liquid slosh around as he tipped it back and forth.

"Oh, and ex-fiancés. Jesus."

He reached for his hat, a dark fedora among the chaos on his dresser.

But he changed direction to pick up a pack of gum first.

Chapter 2 – Balance Can Be Elusive

Socrates patted the side pockets of his coat several times, changing locations until he'd confirmed that each contained a bulge of birdseed. He straightened the brim of his hat and squealed in his door, letting bright hallway light bathe him and chase away from his apartment, if only briefly, some of its shadows.

While pulling the door closed after him, he studied the interplay of red, orange, and yellow patterns of the carpet lining the hallway. The door mechanism clicked, and he pushed against it, trying to turn the knob, then, satisfied that all invaders would be kept at bay, he let go of it and looked toward the stairs.

Like every other time, the squinting just happened reflexively.

Probably from the light leaving no regions outside his apartment free of it.

Definitely from the colors displayed flamboyantly not just by the hallway carpet but by the wallpaper, which favored blues and greens, and the framed paintings and prints on the walls, most of which seemed to silently dedicate their existence to displaying every color imaginable.

He took a few steps before stopping and leaning around a corner where the wall continued as a railing with a wide, flat top piece. And beyond that rail, the foyer below beckoned: a cavernous, colorful space where comfortable furnishings and decor all formed a cheerful refuge under the steady, watchful light from ornamental fixtures hung from the high ceiling in a pattern meant to appear random but giving up its orderly design to anyone that cared to study it for enough time.

Which Socrates had done the first time he'd stood there.

He looked all around but especially at the burgundy couch near the exit.

It was where he'd first seen Wendy.

It was where she was sitting with her cat this Monday morning too.

The cat was mostly just a black smudge on the burgundy fabric except for two shiny green orbs that rarely blinked.

But Wendy's outline was crisp and obvious, her pink sweatshirt and light blue jeans clearly defining her presence and adding yet more buoyant hues to the mix.

Wendy didn't notice him up there, peeking around the corner.

But her cat did, and she seemed content to keep that a secret between her and Socrates.

Dragging his hand along the rail, quietly, he ventured toward the stairway, his other hand in his coat pocket. He faced as much as he could toward the ceiling light fixtures as if he were enjoying sunshine at the beach.

What had begun as slow, careful steps on the short and practical pile of the stair runners, all of them boasting pale purple circles planted onto a regal purple background, became quicker steps until he'd reached the very bottom.

Traveling downward quickly was allowed.

The journey upward required more care.

He wasn't sure exactly why, but that's the policy he'd adopted and wasn't about to abandon.

He'd waited until he was sure that Wendy was looking at him.

Then, he pointed at her, not yet allowing his smile to show.

She made no such effort but covered her smile with one hand.

"Hey, I know you," he said.

He let his smile out, and she dropped her hand, displaying hers and bouncing slightly from her giggling.

He pointed at the cat next and said, "I'm not so sure I know you, though."

Smiling at the still giggling girl, he approached the couch.

"Hello, Wendy."

"Hi, Mr. Lewis."

"Staying inside today?"

When she gave a very modest smirk and turned to look out through the glass doors, so did he. And they both gave only a second of their attention to the rainwater dripping off of the building's awning, the wet roadway beyond, tiny splashes identifying all of the puddles, and the nearly flat wall of brick buildings arrayed unimaginatively across the street, all of them teaming up to eliminate any possibility of seeing the sky.

He'd turned back to her first and watched her sigh as she focused on him instead of the outside world.

"I never get to play outside. You know that."

"Inside is good. More predictable. What's your cat's name again?"

As if she'd needed to be reminded that a cat was lying next to her, she looked down and began rubbing along her back.

The cat continued to gaze silently at Socrates.

"She's Rae. Her whole name is Rae Cat."

"Lovely name."

She continued her gentle adoration of her pet as she looked up at Socrates again, her face quite serious.

"I know now that I called her Rae because my dad called her Stray Cat all the time. I thought he said Rae Cat. I was just little."

Socrates imposed an understanding blankness on his face, barring any smile from appearing.

"Oh. An easy mistake to make when you're just little."

Wendy nodded twice and began fiddling with Rae's ears instead.

"I'm grown up now. But I still like Rae for her name."

Socrates allowed his smile to escape.

But not all of it.

"It's a good name. How old are you again?"

"I'm eight. I don't know how old Rae is."

His smile grew, even as Wendy continued a solemn study of him.

"Of course not. Yes, you're all grown up. Should I think about calling myself Mr. Lewis *Man* to be a little bit like Rae *Cat*?"

First, Wendy's eyes opened wide, then a big smile joined in the fun.

"No, Mr. Lewis! That's silly!"

With both of his hands again verifying the presence of caches of seed in his pockets, Socrates said, "Yes, it surely is. I'm going to feed the birds again. And I'll get some breakfast for myself too."

Her smile had served its purpose and left.

Rae Cat had never smiled.

"Breakfast for the birds too? For both of you?"

Socrates's hands locked onto the seed piles, and he stared down at the child.

With a fresh smile, he said, "Yes. There's some balance in that. Balance can be elusive, you know."

She shrugged and smiled up at him, while Rae continued to gaze at him indifferently.

Still smiling, Socrates tipped his hat toward them both, turned, and began walking toward the exit and the rainy morning awaiting him.

Softly, leaning toward her cat, Wendy said, "'Elusive?' What's that?"

Socrates was five steps away from the couch, about midway between Wendy and the door, when he turned at the sound of rapid footsteps on the stairway.

A woman in jeans and a green sweater was making a rapid descent.

When she turned toward the couch, never slowing, Socrates looked that way too. Wendy was smiling and waving, and Rae had even tipped her head a bit at the sight.

"Hi, Mom. Rae says hi too."

Wendy's mother stopped at the bottom, and she gave them both a quick wave.

"Hello to you both. I'm just stopping down real quick to check on you. I heard voices."

He'd just started smiling at the sight of Wendy again petting a cat that seemed incapable of much other than staring, then he turned back toward the stairway at the sound of Wendy's mother.

"Mr. Lewis, hello. Got a minute?"

He noticed that she hadn't waited for an answer before beginning a determined walk his way.

"Sure. Of course."

Two steps from him, she stopped and smiled, then glanced quickly back at the couch. She faced him again, and her smile evaporated.

When Socrates was sure that her eyes were again locked intently on his, he said, "How have you been?"

"Fine. I just . . ."

Her gaze continued, and she seemed to be concentrating too much to bother with blinking as she tilted her head to her left, then to her right, and she made no attempt to disguise her rapid inhaling as she sampled the air all around Socrates.

With her head upright again, the sniffing ceased, and she gave him an approving smile.

"Well, good. Minty. I don't mean to be rude, Mr. Lewis, but the smell of alcohol on a man's breath probably isn't the best example for a child."

As soon as he realized that he was squinting at her, he erased it as quickly as he could.

"Oh, well, of course. Probably not for a cat either."

She made no effort to curtail her squinting at him. Then, after she'd given him sufficient time to notice it, she turned her head back to her daughter.

"Honey, you do remember that Mr. Lewis is a writer, don't you?"

Wendy nodded. Rae stared.

"And he's so nice to feed the birds all the time. Isn't that all very kind and admirable?"

Wendy nodded and said, "It's very nice, Mom."

Smiling at her daughter, then letting it linger for Socrates to see, she turned back toward him.

"Okay, I just had to sneak that in there. Role models are important, you know."

"I won't claim to know too many things, but I do know that. It's good that you're watching out for the girl."

She nodded while he spoke, then grinned when he'd finished.

She tipped her head back toward the couch and said, "Rae too."

"Yes, of course. Rae Cat."

He tipped his hat to her and said, "Enjoy your morning."

She began turning and said, "I will. Thanks. You too."

Socrates watched for a moment as Wendy's mother walked back toward the stairway, waving again to the girl and cat on the couch. When she began her ascent, he allowed himself only the briefest of glances at her first steps on the carpet runners, the ones crowded with purple circles, then he turned to face the glass.

With both hands, he arranged the brim of his hat, focusing on the sight of the outside world and not on his reflection.

Then, he pushed open the door, felt light water drops carried on the breeze, and stepped out beneath the canopy.

Chapter 3 – Unless You're Already a Madman

The wet wind added a push to the building's self-closing door, and Socrates stepped closer to the thin streams flowing down from clumped fringes along the edge of the fabric awning above him. If its underside had any colors, it kept them hidden in the shadows, and the sky above it wasn't much of a different shade.

Widely-spaced cars, their engines muted by air carrying a full load of moisture, crawled past. Their black tires weren't speedy enough to fan water up behind them, but they managed to squeeze puddles to the sides as they passed. He watched them for a moment as they closed quickly, seeming to hurry the vehicles on their way.

He looked to the right at an empty sidewalk clinging to the brick walls, shrinking and narrowing as it let itself blend into the mist.

But Socrates turned to his left, turned up the collar of his lightweight trench coat, and ventured out toward a familiar destination: a small and reliably unpopular city park several blocks distant.

He noted without opinion that the brim of his hat had begun mimicking the soggy canopy near the door. It sagged as it sponged up the rain, and what couldn't be absorbed quickly enough dripped steadily, the heavier flow changing sides with each step.

With head and brim tipped forward, his view was limited, but he didn't need it. He knew that he was just steps away from the awning of the neighboring building.

So, he tried to find the best locations for his steps through a field of puddles, then took shelter.

The dripping from the hat brim dwindled quickly, then stopped.

His hands were already in his pockets, and he withdrew them at the same time, palms up. His right hand cupped a fair amount of birdseed, and he was careful to avoid spilling any of it. But he had less success with his left hand, which had an undeniable surplus compared to the other and donated some right there for the birds.

"Jesus, it's not just the wind and the fingernails. Everything is in on it—even the damn seed weighting down that side. What chance does a man have all by himself, trying his best to—"

A single loud screech from ahead along the sidewalk caused his hands to shake, spilling only a few seeds, and he tipped his head up enough to see out from under the brim. A large black bird, cutting a streak through the murky gray, was flapping madly, coming from the right, and whooshed into an alley not far ahead.

Socrates hurried to dump the seed back inside, safe again for transport to the park, and walked, sometimes running a few steps, until he could lean past the sharp corner bricks and look into the alley.

Squinting into a region gloomier even than the city street, he darted his eyes around, seeking to locate that bird.

"Huh. You're not looking for seed. You're—"

Something blacker than the alley was rushing right at his face.

"Whoa!"

His hands covered the pockets as he leaned away, then stepped back, and the bird sailed past him, its wings pounding. Socrates watched its flight, angled up and crossing the street, until it merged with the gloom swirling high above the buildings.

He peered around the corner again, straining to see into the early morning dusk, then he took a step to renew his trek to the park but stopped himself when he saw a tiny light.

Just a glint, revealing the presence of something shiny.

"Huh. That explains it. Crows do like shiny things."

His eyes began adjusting to the dismal confines of the alley as he mumbled, "Jesus, I'm still talking to my—"

He saw that there was a figure back there, holding something shiny that glinted from the depths of the alley's night.

* * *

"You again," said the figure with a feminine voice.

Socrates looked each way along the sidewalk, then pointed at his chest as he again faced the shadow speaking to him from the dark.

He started walking toward her, his eyes adjusting enough that he could say softly to himself, "Jesus. Nice legs. Those are—"

"Who sent you? Dammit, please, just tell me already," she said, her voice almost too weak to reverberate off of the wet brick cliffs looming on each side.

Socrates stopped, then groaned a second later at noticing that he was leaning to his left. With a sharp exhale through his nostrils, he forced himself up straight.

"What?" he said. "What did you say?"

He resumed his tentative walk toward her and as the drizzly fog thinned, he saw that she was an attractive woman, younger than him. Her skirt was short, displaying shapely legs ending in high heels. Her resale shop fake fur jacket was soggy, and her hair, long and struggling to retain a few of its waves, was splattered all around.

He'd barely made an effort to see her eyes when she turned her gaze down. His eyes followed, and he saw the scissors that she held. The scissors never moved, but she looked again in his direction.

"It wouldn't kill you to clear this shit up. Which side are you on?"

He'd gotten close enough to see her better, and he smiled before answering.

"Lately, I lean mostly to the left. You can see that? I'm not just imagining it? Before, it was sometimes to the—"

"What?" she said, squinting at him. "No, not that. Oh, you're talking. You're a real person."

She was the first to look down, then they were both observing the sharp, shiny points, parted just a bit and aimed at her abdomen.

"Um, maybe you should put the scissors down."

She didn't move. Didn't speak.

"I, uh, think some bird just tried to tell you that too."

"Yeah," she said. "A bird told me."

With a scoff, she dropped them to clatter into a puddle.

"Why the hell not?"

She shook her head at the sight of it until the water again settled, showing only tiny circles where raindrops fell into it.

"I guess it could tell I didn't really mean to do it this time. It knew I was just sort of thinking it through."

"It, who? That bird? And you didn't mean what?"

She turned enough to face him and wiped under each eye. She blinked slowly, looking his way.

"You really want to know?"

"Sure. Yeah, I want to know. What's bothering you?"

She took her time to look past Socrates, then behind her, deeper into the alley, then back at him.

"I'm exhausted and need to get off the streets. Come back later, and I'll tell you all about it."

He lifted his left hand, pushed back the coat sleeve, and glanced at his watch.

"Like lunchtime, you mean?"

Squinting at him and shaking her head, she said, "No. After dark. Aim for 2:00. I usually hit a slow stretch around last call."

She scoffed, not quite laughing, and said, "Men and their goddamn booze."

Socrates cleared his throat, trying to keep it quiet.

"Uh, I could come back. I don't know for sure, though. Um, what's your name?"

She shook her head and said, "Really, nobody sent you?"

"Huh?"

She shook her head again just once at his perplexed stare, then focused again on the scissors, only the two points visible in the murky puddle where she'd been nudging them around with her toe.

"I'm Miley. You seem nice. But you should probably just stay the hell away from me."

Without waiting for a response, she turned and began to give herself to the mist and gloom, and Socrates just watched her walking away.

Before he'd lost sight of her completely, she turned just enough to see him.

"Unless you're already a madman," she said.

Again, not waiting for any comment he might have, she turned and resumed her walk. Socrates listened to her heels on the pavement and watched the sway of her hips until she was gone, carried away by clouds of raindrops and shadows.

He took one step forward, eyes still searching for her.

Then, he took a few more backwards.

He glanced around to confirm that he was the only soul left in that alley, then he turned to walk back toward the street.

Chapter 4 – Fighting Fruitlessly

Holding his hat brim and leaning into the wind and rain, Socrates approached a solitary wooden park bench, one whose weathered gray planks hadn't been splashed with fresh paint for many years. It faced toward his left, where empty train tracks drew straight iron lines in each direction, evenly spaced lampposts keeping them company on the far side.

Behind the bench, an open expanse of grass, yellowed and starved from the heat of a summer that had just passed, backed up to spotty trees and shrubs. And beyond that growth, brick buildings crowded themselves together. Most windows were still dark, and a zigzag pattern of rusty metal was bolted in place to offer its inhabitants a physical escape.

Socrates sighed and turned his back to the grass and trees and solemn structures, and he didn't bother looking past the asphalt walkway, having seen the tracks and barren scrabble beyond them enough times.

He looked down to the pavement near his right side.

Then, near his left.

He found that he was leaning that way, so he scowled and looked to his right, into the wind and along a wet footpath devoid of anyone walking or running or even passing through with food carts on their way to a more favored park.

"Damn wind. Always the goddamn wind."

He eased himself down onto the wet boards, gave the tracks one unfocused glance, then shook his head as he looked at his lap.

Forcing his voice into a higher pitch, he tipped his head both ways repeatedly and said, "'Which side are you on?'"

He scoffed.

"Couldn't she see? I don't know, but it should be obvious. Left. Almost always to the left. She had to see it."

He cast his gaze past the tracks and their unlit lamps, past the rough fields where buildings had been razed and never rebuilt, and stared without focus into the gray sky just above the horizon.

His right pocket was first to get scooped out and its cargo of birdseed tossed down in front of him. The left pocket didn't have to wait long before it got mostly emptied too.

He noticed the birds descending for the free meal, but he didn't give them much of his attention.

But he did notice that he wasn't sitting up quite straight.

He groaned and forced himself up, then said, "Jesus, even when I'm sitting."

Turning down only his eyes, he saw that all of the pigeons had suspended their feast and were studying him silently. Their unreadable eyes concealed thoughts that would never be known, he realized.

"What? Never seen a man fighting fruitlessly against the merciless wind before? All of you should know about the wind. You're some kind of experts, right?"

At the sound of light squeaking carried toward him on the wind, he continued lecturing the birds while turning enough to see.

"Just eat your damn breakfast."

He nodded at the sight of a street vendor cruising his way with a wagon for dishing up hot dogs.

"I sure as hell will."

Chapter 5 – Not Just for Cats

He pulled eagerly on the heavy glass door behind him and was surprised when the brisk wind added a boost, causing it to slam noisily. Socrates turned his head quickly to look around the lobby, and he saw Wendy and Rae seated on the same couch but at the other end than earlier.

Although Wendy had lowered an open book and was already smiling at him, he still took a moment to look around at the bright colors on every surface as he brushed rainwater off of the sleeves of his coat, then he began the short walk toward her.

"Hi, Mr. Lewis. Did you feed the birds?"

Before answering, he watched for a moment as the cat tried to squirm out of Wendy's grasp, but she kept her pinned snugly by her side.

"Yeah, I sure did. Um, I think maybe Rae Cat wants to get loose for a while."

The cat kept up her escape attempts as Wendy looked quickly out through the wet windows and doors.

"Oh. Probably you, too, huh?"

Wendy let out a deep sigh before again looking toward Socrates. While holding his gaze, she raised her arm mechanically, freeing Rae, who quickly jumped to the floor.

"My mom says I'm safer inside," she said as she let her arm fall.

"She's right. Your cat is too."

Both of them devoted some time to watching Rae strut silently toward a nearby upholstered chair, then jump up onto its seat. From there, she clawed up onto the back, then jumped down behind it, out of their sight.

A second later, she trotted off to the side, where a table against the wall, finished to look like white marble, had a lower shelf a short distance above the floor.

Rae wiggled her way under there but not completely.

Her black tail extended out, and it waved around in random directions.

"I don't think Rae cares about being safe, Mr. Lewis."

Still watching the cat, he said, "And why do you suppose that is?"

Rae snapped her tail into the shadows beneath the low shelf, then Socrates and Wendy watched two black paws come out the side, pads up, and Rae pulled herself out and stood.

She stared at them for only a second, then she pranced off for more.

Socrates turned back to Wendy just in time to see her shrug.

"She's curious about things?"

Socrates gave the girl a squint, then they both watched Rae Cat leap onto the back of a couch close up against a wall. From there, she stood and pawed at a wide painting of a field of wildflowers, all beneath a brooding sky scratched every which way from daggers of lightning.

"Huh. That sounds right. But remember that curiosity . . . um, I mean, that's not just for cats."

Wendy gave her cat a brief glance, then looked up again at Socrates, her face showing no hint of whether she agreed or disagreed.

After a pause, she only shrugged.

"Okay," he said, "have a nice day."

"Bye, Mr. Lewis."

They both gave Rae a few more moments as her audience, witnessing her jumping down from the couch only to race full speed and launch herself behind another chair.

"Huh."

Then, Socrates left the girl and her cat for the stairs.

Chapter 6 – Nothing About Hookers

It had to be done without any obvious signs, he knew. Each step had to be placed at a measured pace, not skipping any of the treads and certainly never showing any hesitation.

He scanned the first step quickly, his eyes darting from left to right, then back. As many times as he could.

Counting the lighter purple circles.

Finding just the right place for his shoe to evenly divide them, leaving the same number of them on each side.

He knew that he'd come close to placing the step accurately, but there wasn't enough time to verify at least once, or ideally twice, that his placement was correct.

Because there could be no delay in beginning the motion of the other foot.

Eyes were watching. Probably from that couch.

A girl.

And her cat.

The cat was always watching.

So, he forced his eyes to the next step, and he tried to not give in to the overwhelming difficulty of it all because each step's carpet piece was different.

Whoever had installed the damn things had had no sense of order, cutting out pieces willy-nilly so that no two of them had the same beginning and end.

And worse, regardless of their arrangement, every circle was a different size.

He'd tried to memorize each step's pattern, and he could sometimes come close to dividing the light purple circles well enough, at least by count.

But they lacked consistency of diameter, so the real challenge had quickly become to place each step so that the total area of lighter purple dot circles on the left matched the total area on the right.

Each step, each rapid view left to right, required instant estimates of numbers of circles, the areas of each, and the sums on each side of where he couldn't hesitate to place his step. Because someone—likely a girl and a cat, at least—might be analyzing his gait, and they'd see too easily that he was failing.

That he couldn't possibly know if he'd ever succeeded.

They might not see it, but he knew that it was all a harsh indication that math didn't like him.

Mostly, it was an unending reminder that his leaning to the left always hindered his efforts beyond repair.

Even something as simple as traversing a stairway.

Up, though. Not down.

That's just the way it was.

The steps won another round, and Socrates began the journey toward his door. But even on that level expanse, he felt the incessant leaning, with or without wind to blame, dogging him the entire way. But his breaths were calmer and deeper, and he didn't need to study the red, orange, and yellow elements of the carpet along that route.

Early on, he'd accepted that he couldn't possibly tally the items and areas for the full length and width of the hallway with each step, then know where to rest the soles of his shoes so as to make some surgical division of it all with each and every step.

If it had been divided into neat rectangles, maybe.

But just one single giant piece of carpet?

No. He just couldn't know.

But the jumble of sharp hues was amusing and refreshing until he'd reached his doorway, passed through, then began closing the door.

With his back to his living space, he watched as the sliver of colors and bright light narrowed then vanished as he locked it all out.

*　*　*

Dividing his attention between a blank sheet collecting dust where it waited in his typewriter and whatever amount of attention was needed to perch his coat on the back of the other chair at the table, Socrates hurried to get it hanging in a balanced way, then picked up the whiskey bottle.

"Jesus, who's been drinking all of this?"

He laughed and grabbed the empty glass, then poured a fair amount. Half of it disappeared quickly, and he set it down, already reaching for the closest coat pocket with his other hand.

Digging around in the deepest part of it, he shook his head and pulled out a few birdseeds.

"Huh. Pigeons got cheated this time."

He found the other pocket totally empty, and he left the straggler seeds on the table beside the typewriter. That hand got left on the tabletop, too, and he drummed his fingers a few times.

"Sure, why not? What else am I doing at 2:00 am?"

He looked again at the typewriter.

"Sure as hell won't be writing."

Leaving the bottle and glass and blank sheet, he walked into his bedroom, glanced in the mirror on his way past it, and stopped near the nightstand next to his bed.

Lifting up the clock, its wire dangling behind it, he held it close and tapped the controls, setting a wakeup time of 1:45. He set it down next to the book, stared at it for a few seconds, then frowned and quickly reset it back to 8:00.

"Why would I even think of going back to that damn alley? If there's a good reason, I sure as hell don't know it. Some suicidal hooker in an alley. Jesus."

He scoffed and picked up the book, then held it up close, flipping through it. Light wind blew in, leaning him.

Searching the pages, reading some passages and skipping others, he corrected his posture only to have the wind undo his efforts each time.

"Huh."

He snapped it closed, then tapped it on his forehead a few times.

"You're no help at all. Not this time."

The book found its place next to the clock, centered and spaced a uniform distance from it after careful nudging.

"Nothing in there about hookers. There's a whole lot philosophical about hookers."

He pointed down at it, grinning.

"All you have to do is ask me."

He gave the philosopher Socrates a chance to respond, then he pointed at the book again.

"But not right now. Time to get to work."

* * *

He stared at the blank sheet, and it offered not a single seed for anything to germinate. It was the inside of a table tennis ball, a sky packed with snow, a patch of carpet bleached clean of purple circles.

He knew that even a first word, whether it would survive or get edited into oblivion, would help lead to the rest. But no amount of staring summoned it.

The quiet room welcomed the tapping of his fingernails on the whiskey bottle, keeping as consistent of a pace as he could manage, starting with the little finger and progressing through the rest.

Always in order.

Always seeking the correct height on the bottle to produce the same tone of clicks, depending on the relative surplus or scarcity of liquid inside.

And that bottle nearly tipped when he jerked his hand at the sound of his phone ringing on the other side of the typewriter.

He steadied the bottle first, then picked up and tapped the phone.

"Well, it's—"

"Dad, you said you were going to call Mom."

"I don't know that I actually said that, Lynnie. I remember saying—"

"Fine. Say it now, then. When are you going to call her?"

He watched his right hand abandon the bottle for the glass, which he picked up and held close. Ready.

"I don't know. Real soon, probably. There's work that I have to—"

"Right. Work. I don't even believe that."

"Jesus, Lynnie, I—"

He froze himself, his face locked in a tight wince while he listened to the silence from his phone.

"I mean, really, I'm right here at the typewriter."

He heard her scoff, and it brought him a smile.

"Still with the typewriter. Really, come on already."

"I lost my work once. You remember that. Never again."

"Right. Perfectly safe. Hey, maybe Mom would be happy to hear from you. You don't know."

"Well, it would be a surprise. She's never said that."

"Have you ever asked her?"

"Well, no, but should I have to? If it's so—"

"Alright. I tried. Told her I would. Bye."

He was holding both the phone and glass close, and the phone took a ride out to where he could see that Lynnie had cut the conversation.

The phone found its place on the table, and the glass was about to deliver its cargo when the phone rang out again. He flinched and spilled a few drops on the blank sheet, then he frowned at the phone, tapped it, and held it to his left ear.

"Jesus, Mara. I'm just getting in a groove here with a piece that—"

"Sure you are. Look, I had to make a decision. You have till the end of the week. Get something decent to me or you're out."

"Out of your good favor?" he said, grinning.

"You know, maybe you should be writing comedy stuff. Maybe cartoons or something. No, Socrates. Out as in out. Got it?"

The glass had closed the distance, about ready to tip.

"Jesus. Yeah. Alright, before the end of—"

"If you're drinking, stop. Just stop."

He reached the phone far enough away that he knew it could see the scowl he was directing its way, then he set it down. But he kept his hand close, staring at it.

It kept quiet.

Still keeping watch of the phone, he set down the glass, then looked at it, snatched it back up, and drank it all.

Then, both phone and empty glass rested comfortably on his kitchen table, each as close to the same distance from the typewriter as he could determine.

After glaring at the paper for a moment, he checked the watch on his left wrist.

"Oh, well, the work can wait."

Reaching across the table, he pulled two plastic containers closer, keeping them butted up against each other.

He leaned forward, checking the height of the contents in each one.

Satisfied, he uncapped the one on the left and poured some of its seed into the left pocket of his coat. He repeated it for the right side.

The containers were again resting in their place, across the table and touching, their insides forming one common horizontal line.

He gave the speechless sheet a sour look, then flicked it once with a finger before pushing his chair away from the table and standing.

But he waited there, studying his next great work.

"Off to a good start."

Chapter 7 – She Wants More Adventures

Wearing his fedora and coat, pockets packed with pigeon food, Socrates paused at the door to look around his dim apartment. Through the doorway to the kitchen, where he'd shut off the overhead light, he saw that the paper had still managed to remain the brightest item that could be seen.

"Jesus, you're mocking me, aren't you?"

He sighed and let himself out into the hallway, one hand raised to partially cover his eyes. The door mechanism clunked its assurance that it would keep out marauders, and he looked down at the staggering number of red, orange, and yellow components plastered onto a background content to draw little glory for itself.

And he gave none of it any acclaim.

A few steps later, he leaned out and saw the empty burgundy couch—no Wendy and no Rae Cat.

He continued until he'd reached the top of the stairway, where he scanned the descending rectangles of light purple circles pinned to a darker purple canvas.

And he knew that they didn't matter either—not on the way down.

He hurried to the bottom, then hiked across the clean tile floor to the building's glass doors, and he stopped there, looking out at a world still gloomy at midday.

"Jesus, is it ever going to stop with the damn rain?"

The canopy's soggy fringe hung straight down, most strands with a heavy water bead at their ends. They took turns releasing those larger drops, adding them to the uniform flow collected and directed to the edge by the sloping fabric.

"Damn birds have to eat, too, right?"

He tipped his head, ignoring the rain beyond the glass and focusing instead on his reflection. He'd already felt it, but seeing it, getting that concrete confirmation, was always a—

A meow from behind him and high above the floor spun him around, and his eyes reflexively trained on a moving black shape—Rae.

With some effort, he differentiated Wendy's pink and light blue clothing colors from the wall's blue and green colors and patterns behind her.

He nodded at seeing that she stood almost perfectly midway between two paintings on the wall behind her.

Just half a step to the right would be better, though.

He shook his head and pointed at the cat, who was more than an arm's length from Wendy and walking along the railing's top piece on the second floor's balcony.

"Wendy, better keep an eye on that Rae Cat."

She didn't keep her eyes on the cat and instead, peered over the railing down at Socrates.

"I am. But she's okay."

"Is she safe? It wouldn't be good for her to fall off. Don't want to lose her."

Wendy tipped her head while studying Rae's progress along the rail, carefully and deliberately placing her paws on the smooth surface. Wendy straightened up and held Socrates's gaze again.

"She might be old, Mr. Lewis. We don't know. Maybe she wants more adventures."

He knew that his jaw had gone slack, and he knew that Wendy had noticed and was watching him quite seriously.

"More adventures?" he said softly to himself.

Then, he smiled up at the young girl, eliciting a bright smile from her too.

"You're right, Wendy. Maybe at any age, adventures are a good thing?"

She didn't lose her smile, and she gave him a few quick nods before again looking after her cat, who was still making skillful, confident progress along the polished handrail, high above the tile floor of the lobby.

Wendy wouldn't notice it, he realized, but he tipped his hat toward her anyway. Then, he gave it another quick tip toward the adventurous feline, who had turned her green eyes to spy down on him.

And she froze there, with one paw locked in the air.

Socrates froze, too, staring, then he said, "Huh."

He turned to face the glass and remembered just where he'd left off with his exam before a meow had pulled him off course: his reflection.

And his leaning.

To the left. Almost always to the left.

Not breaking a determined stare into his mirrored eyes, he scooped a small amount of seed from the left coat pocket, passed it to his right hand, and dumped it into the right pocket.

It helped. A little.

"That might be a more permanent solution than whiskey, I suppose. I sure as hell won't eat the seed and throw things out of whack. Whiskey, though? Huh."

He gave the door a shove and passed through, for the moment dry beneath the awning and hearing the relentless splatting above.

The street toward the right appeared to be poked into a gray veil where it vanished in the distance. The lines of traffic blurred into lumpy dark threads being pulled in and out of that veil.

He turned to his left, put his hands in the coat pockets, and stepped out into the light rain.

Only two steps later, he stopped and whipped around at the sound of frantic flapping of wings behind him.

The sounds ended abruptly, and he looked back, then up, then across the street.

Then, up higher across the street, he scanned all around until he fixed on three pigeons on a ledge, not a single one of them aware that he even existed.

He kept his eyes on them until he turned to resume his walk, then he looked ahead, turned up his collar, and began a more spirited walk toward the park.

Where he knew some pigeons that not only were aware that he existed but were likely wondering just what the hell was taking him so long.

Chapter 8 – Their Maddening Ways

He'd dumped his coat across a chair in the kitchen, but the fedora remained where he'd installed it as he watched the curtains of his open bedroom window get tossed around by the wind.

With an intentionally loud scoff, as if the window would take notice, he forced himself to stand straighter, then looked down at the clock, which showed 12:07.

He reached for it but changed direction before touching it, lifting up the book instead. Standing in the light wind, leaning away from it, he opened the book, read a little, turned a few pages, read some more, then snapped it shut and set it back down.

He chuckled and said, "You really didn't know anything, did you? You were a bum."

His hand was still close to the book, so he adjusted its position relative to the clock, then tapped his fingers on it a few times.

Little finger first, then proceeding through the others.

"A bum like me. Shit, there are no books about me, though."

He abandoned the real Socrates to stand straight up and gaze out the window.

"So, that cat likes adventures, huh? That's a smart cat. Or maybe she's just a reckless little beast. One way to find out."

He let out a single deep sigh, then fussed with the clock until the alarm showed 1:45.

After backing away from it a few steps, he turned to face his mirror and confronted the image he knew that he'd find: a man leaning to the left.

With a snort, he snapped his left arm up in front of him, quickly detached the wristwatch, and even more quickly applied it to the right.

Before checking the results, still looking down, he shook his head and frowned.

"Jesus, I'm just now thinking of that?"

Then, he looked and saw that the corrective action had had almost no success.

"Well, it didn't make it worse."

He poured some whiskey and held up the glass, aiming to give himself a toast. Instead, he jutted it out as far to the right as he could.

And he grinned at the reflection grinning back and standing tall and straight, one eye on each side of a shoestring suspending a ring that he knew had been much shinier and possessing more hope for the future not too far in the past.

Only a couple of tired decades in the past.

He let his grin fade, then turned to see the open window and its invading wind beyond the half-full glass in his outstretched hand.

"Wind be damned. I have whiskey."

*　*　*

The wind wasn't impressed, so he stared it down as he finished the glass. With the bottle in his other hand, he ambled out of his bedroom and into the kitchen, eyes on the blank sheet the entire way.

Before sitting, he placed his phone to the left of the typewriter and the glass and bottle to the right. Then, he adjusted all of them.

With his left hand poised near the keyboard and the back of his right hand near the bottle, giving it a series of fingernail taps, he stared at the grand manuscript that would soon appear.

Then, his phone screamed, he nearly tipped the bottle but caught it by the neck, and he leaned over to see "Valerie" on the caller ID.

He frowned and let it ring some more.

Then, he picked it up and tapped it.

"Val. I was just about to call you."

She was sitting on a plush couch among decorative pillows, dressed well, and with admirable posture. Her home was bright, colorful, and decorated richly.

"I bet. Hi, um . . . well, Socrates. Sure."

"Thanks. I do like that name. Feels right."

His hand found the glass.

"Lynnie told me she called you."

"Yes, she did call. She seems to be doing well these days."

"She's doing fine, especially with school. Are you?"

He let go of the glass, splaying his fingers out, but he kept his hand near it.

"Yeah. I'm writing, and, uh, it's coming along."

He tipped up the blank sheet, then let it drop.

"And, um, I'm finding some success in leaving all sorts of things around here to their maddening ways. Especially the damn dresser."

"We did talk about that. You mean, um, not perfectly organized?"

"Oh, uh, yeah. That's what I meant."

"Well, I can't talk long. Lynnie told me you were writing. I just wanted to tell you that if you got your writing career going again, that would, I mean, that could . . . well, that would be good."

"Oh, um, yeah. That sure could be good. Uh, what I'm working on is big. Like, a life-changing kind of thing. It kind of sums up life pretty accurately. Mine anyway."

He smirked without a sound as he flicked the paper, then reached for the glass.

"What's it about?"

"Oh, you know, I can't really say. It's, uh, better if it hits you all at once."

"Fine. I still have a subscription. They'll publish it soon?"

He laughed as he elevated the glass.

"They damn well better. It'll blow up that damn magazine. Probably get me a few choice job offers too."

"That would be good. Are you having hot dogs for lunch too? Yeah, she told me about that."

He smiled down at the whiskey that he was swirling around.

"Oh, that's just for breakfast. I'll find something else for lunch."

"Well, I'm about to have my own lunch, so . . ."

"Okay. Thanks for calling, Val."

"Bye . . .uh, Socrates."

Still smiling, he set the phone down while raising the glass up. But before taking a drink, he looked through the dark liquid at the clear sheet that had been waiting a while.

He downed the whiskey in a single gulp, then held the glass out to set it near the bottle. He didn't set it down, though—just held it closer to the blank sheet.

He looked from the empty paper to the empty glass and back to the empty paper.

"Huh. That's something."

Chapter 9 – Her Name Is Miley

"Holy Jesus. Why so goddamn loud?"

With the alarm buzzing angrily, Socrates fumbled around in the dark room, finally found the clock, wrestled it into submission, then located the kill switch and returned the room to silence.

Except for his agitated breaths.

He held it up to confirm the time and saw 1:45 in very light orange, its weak attempt at color barely surviving in the cave of darkness all around it.

The clock got set down clumsily and tipped to point its numbers at the ceiling, the two dots blinking each second as if sending up a distress signal.

He left the clock and switched on the small lamp, which right away reminded him that he'd planned to put a higher wattage bulb in it. But it was enough to transform it all from black to gray.

A lazy folding back of blankets freed his legs, and he swung them out and let them drop, his bare feet hitting the cold floor when he sat up. From there, he stretched his arms to his sides and yawned, then raked his fingers around on his scalp.

With eyes reluctant to be pried open, he checked the window, which was closed, and saw thin lines of rainwater creeping from top to bottom.

"Again with the goddamn rain? Jesus."

He scoffed at it and stood, then shuffled over to face his mirror.

But he kept his eyes shut.

Grinning in the near darkness, he reached out and didn't miss with a light tap to the ring, setting his pendulum in motion.

He let the smile get a head start, then he cracked his eyes open just enough to snag the bottle, which he pulled back and held against his chest.

He thanked himself silently for using a white shoestring since it couldn't hide in the shadows like most other stuff on the dresser and all around his room, and he opened his eyes.

The bottle went to his left hand, then was shot out all the way, and he leaned with it.

But the string kept up a quick pace, and it had gone through a few passes before he'd gotten the bottle all the way out.

He quickly changed hands, jabbed it out to the right, and tried to match with the swing to the right.

The string was cycling too quickly. He'd never come close.

With the bottle back in the left hand, he locked himself in place and watched as the glistening ring swung quickly and spun slowly, suspended on a shoestring, hung from a mirror's frame to gauge the leaning of a man holding a bottle of whiskey.

At about 2:00 am.

He looked up toward the ceiling.

"Huh. Maybe a longer string?"

He focused again on the ring as it moved left to right, all the while spinning too.

"Sweet Jesus, I'm losing it. Didn't that hooker ask if I was a madman?"

He aborted the laughter before it had a chance and set the bottle down quietly.

Serious eyes studied him from the gray mirror. Both on the left side of the string.

But right then, he didn't care.

"Miley. Her name is Miley."

*　　*　　*

Dressed and attempting to stay straight, Socrates walked from the gloom of his bedroom to the gray of his kitchen and directly to his coat on one of the chairs.

He slipped that on, checked the pockets out of habit, found them empty, then looked toward the two plastic containers of seed at the far edge of the table.

All he did was scoff at them.

"No way. No pigeons to feed this time of night. They're not that stupid."

He stared a second longer.

"Um, I mean, adventurous."

He took a step toward the door, then jerked himself to a stop.

"Oh, I do need that hat, though."

He checked the watch on his right wrist as he hurried back into the bedroom, then again left for the door.

But he stopped himself at the kitchen table.

"Oh, yeah, I might need that too."

He continued walking through his shadowy apartment.

"Jesus, wasn't I going to stop talking to myself?"

He shrugged, pulled in the door, and winced at the brightness which never relented—a lobby with its own array of suns that never set in their own sky.

Chapter 10 – Looking for Trouble

Socrates only barely focused on any of the purple circles on the steps as he hurried down over them, skipping a few. He spent most of his time watching the couch, the comfortable burgundy residence, it sometimes seemed, of Wendy and her cat.

But they weren't there, and he knew why.

It was just shy of 2:00 am.

He continued on to the glass doors, held his hands up as shields to filter out reflections of the daylight always present in the building's lobby, and saw the fabric ceiling out there flapping quietly, its waterfall rarely showing any breaks as it splashed on the concrete sidewalk.

He turned back around and looked up to the balcony, where Wendy had looked down at him and Rae Cat had played daredevil on a balance beam high above the floor.

Both of them speaking to him of adventures.

The cat offering him a live demonstration.

"Sleep, Wendy. Don't go looking for trouble like that Rae Cat of yours."

He frowned as he kept staring up at the empty space.

"Or like me."

A quick spin left him facing the glass and a clear reflection of a leaning man.

He groaned and said, "Could be worse. But it still needs help."

He turned to his right, enough to lean his left shoulder into the offending mirror, and he slipped and scraped his shoes to his left, forcing himself to stand straight.

"Another impermanent solution," he said with a scoff. "Can't stand here all goddamn night."

He reached into his right coat pocket as he looked down and partly withdrew the whiskey bottle.

"Yet, a portable and provably helpful solution, though also temporary, is always at hand."

He let the portable and helpful but temporary solution retreat to the depths of the pocket.

"Shit. Forgot the glass, though."

He checked the fingernails on both hands, then pushed open the door and turned up his collar as he exited the building.

*   *   *

Light rain fell and ran off of his hat much like it was a personal fabric awning that he toted along with him. The city streets were quiet except for varying amounts of drops plinking into puddles as he approached then passed them.

He stopped at the entrance to the alley where he'd talked with Miley, remembering that it had been quite dark in there then, even in the day—from the low, dark clouds and incessant rain.

But at night, almost the dead middle of it, there was no light lurking anywhere.

Not even a glint off of a suicide weapon.

"What the hell am I doing here?"

He adjusted his collar and began a measured walk into the shadows, then splashed to a quick stop at a low growl right behind him.

He listened, frozen in place with one shoe in a puddle, as the unseen beast taunted him with a soft roar like a mournful musical note that some lonely vocalist held far too long for dramatic effect.

"Jesus, what now?"

He spun around, the growling stopped, and he looked everywhere that had light for looking, and he tried not to think too much about those areas where night had packed itself in too solidly.

But there was only soft drizzling in a dark alley which led to the quiet street that seemed committed to remaining devoid of traffic.

Scoffing, he said, "That was Rae Cat. Had to be. She wants to steal part of my adventure."

He spun back around, adjusted his collar, and resumed his walk but with the expectation of something other than Wendy's cat pouncing on him from behind.

Still, he managed to smile about it.

"Not tonight, little black cat."

Chapter 11 – That Old Serpent

The alley seemed to be cooking up its own night, one several shades darker than the street Socrates had just left, and it welcomed him in deeper with a cool embrace. The sound of his steps, sometimes with a flourish of splashes, couldn't carry too far in air so dense with water.

Still, he ignored his tipped stature to look ahead, farther into the gloom, and saw a figure near the brick wall. Something was catching bits of streetlight that dared to venture along the same path as he, and he tried cocking his head each way to see if it was scissors in Miley's hand.

Or perhaps it was a knife this time.

No, it was only a thin stream of rainwater coursing through a hole in an umbrella held above the head of a hooker.

Alone in the alley.

And forsaking income just to wait for him.

A few more steps, intentionally hushed by keeping the soles of his shoes close to the pavement, sometimes wading through the standing water, got him close. But she still hadn't turned to acknowledge his presence.

Sighing, and keeping any groaning as hushed as his walk toward her, he pressed his left shoulder into the wet bricks, then shuffled his feet in closer, forcing his frame upright.

In the near total darkness, he squinted and tried to somehow focus his eyes more effectively, but he mostly recognized only the steady stream of water falling to the ground and the smooth skin of her cheek as she looked directly out from the wall.

And her legs. Her legs were the most visible part of the whole scene.

He cleared his throat softly, then said, "Hey, um, you—"

"You ever shoot?" she said.

He stared for a second, trying to see her eyes, but she seemed to be more interested in the equally wet and filthy bricks across the narrow alleyway, though they hid themselves well.

"Sure, I do shots. Mostly, I sip. I like to savor it."

"No, not that. Like, at a range. I used to shoot with my dad. You know what the wind can do, right? Especially if it's a long shot?"

He tipped his head, trying to get her to look at him and when she didn't, he looked behind him, toward the street, then back at her.

"Sure. Yeah, even a small breeze. But what does that have to—"

"Doesn't take much, does it?"

"Not much. Um, what are you talking about?"

At the sound of a police car whooping its siren twice behind him, back on the street, he saw her look past him, so he turned enough to look too. The car rolled past quietly, its lights flashing at a precise rhythm.

He snapped around again and saw her face and legs bathed in blue, and she was still gazing past him until the light had faded and their night tightened back up around them.

When she reached for his hand, he watched but didn't try to evade her grip, even when she began a modest pull to get him moving.

"Come on. I can't get busted again."

"You've been arrested?"

"Been a while. It seems that handing out freebies fixes things like that. Live and learn."

"Um, 'handing?'"

She scoffed and said, "Yeah, they'll settle for that. You're listening. That's good."

Still holding his hand, she began walking into the darker depths, and he followed, not fighting her but not trying to catch up either.

The light from a single bulb, above a doorway three steps down, lit their path, and he gave the brick walls to either side only the briefest of glances, then kept looking at his hand in hers.

And her legs, which were expertly placing her heels only in the infrequent and meager puddle-free areas.

She spoke over her shoulder, still pulling him along.

"It isn't classy but hell, it's out of the rain."

He laughed once and said, "And away from lions and things."

She stopped, and he caught himself before bumping her.

When she turned, the light from behind him somehow managed to light only her eyes, leaving the rest a silhouette that blocked the glowing bulb behind her.

"You got your own weird shit going on, don't you?"

She turned, stepped lightly down the steps, and yanked open the door, inviting outside only slightly more light that seemed to carry clouds of smoke along with it.

Trying to see ahead inside, he said, "Don't we all. What does shooting have to do with—"

"Show some patience, will you? Not everything has a one-word explanation. Inside."

She took one step through the doorway, and he felt the warmth of her hand. And he noticed the softness of it.

* * *

He found himself stretched out, one hand pulled into the dank interior while the other snagged behind them the door to the alley. He closed it with a loose rattle then let go of it, allowing himself to get drawn farther inside.

When she stopped, he stopped, and they both looked around.

"Lovely," he said to himself.

A short, cramped bar, ashen and shadowy, crouched along the far wall, every stool covered by a patron in a black or gray coat, a black or gray hat, or both. Cramped booths and tables lurked to the left and

48

right, some containing eyes watching them from beneath hat brims or above glasses or bottles.

He hurried a look down and saw the folded umbrella hanging from her hand, dripping into a small puddle on a stained concrete floor.

Most seats were taken, and Socrates made an effort to see what slice of the population spent the early morning hours in a place that he never knew existed. But every face that he checked was either turned away, or down, or obscured in some other fashion. They'd all dressed to camouflage themselves, none offering any clear boundary between their outlines and the shade into which they'd been planted.

His study was aborted when he got coaxed to the right, and he saw their destination: the only vacant booth on that side. Vacant of patrons but not the leavings of whoever had just used it: plates, bottles, ripped and soiled napkins, even some loose change.

She let go of his hand and claimed the right side, so he took the left. He started clearing and organizing the tabletop, beginning by sweeping it all to the left. He'd just begun addressing the disarray of coins, about to divide them into two camps of equal numbers and ideally, equal areas, when he was stopped by her hand bumping one of his.

He looked up to see her waiting for his eyes to find hers.

"Alright. You know that wind is a problem. That—"

"I cuss at my window when the damn wind comes in, so I know what—"

"Will you just listen a minute? Shit, you just keep—"

She looked from his eyes to his left shoulder, which he'd just pressed into the wall. And he was shifting and sliding on the seat, setting himself up straight.

When she saw that he'd finished and was again giving her his full attention, she shook her head at him, looked around the room quickly, then held his gaze, her eyes clear and intense.

"Alright, let's try this again. If you pray, then—hey, what's your name?"

"Um, my real name?"

Squinting, she said, "Any name."

She rolled her eyes and added, "Give me your fake one."

"Socrates."

She scoffed and said, "Perfect. I don't look like I ever studied philosophy, do I?"

He didn't fight it when his eyes, all on their own, tipped way down to see all of Miley's exposed skin above her low-cut sweater, which seemed to be attracting more than its share of the bar's neon light.

Still looking there, he coughed once and said, "Well, uh, you . . . you look like—"

"Look like a hooker. Think I don't know that?"

He tore his eyes away and focused on hers instead, but winced from her serious glare.

"Well, you probably—"

"Rhetorical question. I did read some philosophy books. On my own—no fancy college bullshit. Do you ask God for things, Socrates?"

"Uh, not lately. Not since I was lost once as a kid."

"Did praying help?"

"Not a damn bit."

She squinted and said, "So, you're still lost out there?"

He grinned, still holding her gaze, and said, "Not out there anyway. Alright, maybe it helped."

"Where did that happen?"

He blew out a sharp breath, trying to keep it quiet, and made sure both palms were flat on an area of the table that he'd cleared.

"It was only in a city park, but I was just a kid, and it seemed like a giant wilderness to me. I thought all kinds of things were going to eat me. Bears and lions and vultures and—"

"Vultures? Really?"

He tried to knot up the wood surface in his fists, his fingernails scratching against it.

"Some kind of big birds. How should I know? I was just little."

"Whoa, easy. Obviously, they didn't eat you."

He forced his palms into the wood, twisting them, trying to clean up some spots he'd seen there.

"But they could have. It was rainy, I fell off this little wall I was on, off to the right, and I must have hit my head because when they found me, I didn't even know my name. I remember how that felt: I tried to talk, but I couldn't find the words, and I—"

"Hey, it's okay now. Easy, alright?"

His breaths had quickened, and he noticed her dip her eyes down to watch his hands, so he forced them to be still.

"Look, you were just a kid. You're fine now. Anyway, if you do decide to chat with God again, don't ask for anything. That's all I'm saying."

He let out a deep breath, then rolled his shoulders up and around a couple of times and laced his fingers.

"Huh? Isn't that the point?"

She shook her head a few times, staring into each of his eyes for a moment.

"I asked for something, and I got it. I just wanted some kind of fresh idea, something maybe no one thought about or sure didn't talk about. Something like that. Thought I'd write a book about it. I never should have asked."

"Why not? What's wrong with asking?"

"Because I got that idea."

She raised a hand and tapped on the side of her head, and Socrates leaned to get a better look at her manicured nails.

"It got dug in deep, like a twisty hot drill bit. And now, I can't even—"

A man appeared beside their booth and leaned toward her. He was dressed all in black—wrinkled, shabby dress clothes, all wet from rain. While he whispered to her, she nodded, her eyes on Socrates.

He retreated somewhere behind Socrates, who had never gotten a good look at his face.

"That was kind of poetic. That drill bit thing," he said.

"Thanks. We have to go. The boss is coming. Bet you don't want to pay the going rate for my time, do you?"

He leaned away from the wall and reached for his back pocket.

"Uh, I probably could. Maybe if we were to—"

She held up a hand, showing delicate skin and only a tasteful amount of jewelry. Socrates stopped and let himself slump back into the wall.

"Then, I'd hate you like the rest."

"You hate them? All of them?"

"Look around," she said with a quick snarl. "You want them all lined up, cash in their hands, about to stick it to you?"

"Jesus, no. But I'm, I mean, it's different because—"

"Rhetorical question."

She smiled. The first he'd seen from her.

"You madman."

*   *   *

She lifted her umbrella and began scooting out of the booth, her eyes still on him but her smile fading. He hurried onto his feet beside her, and she again took his hand, leading him toward the exit with the point of her umbrella helping to clear a path through the few patrons, faces mostly unseen, who were huddled around by the door, laughing and finishing drinks.

The door squealed open into a light rainfall, darker than before until their eyes had time to adjust. She took him up the concrete stairway and popped open the tattered umbrella. He took a few quick steps to get under it with her, and they began a splashing walk toward the relative brightness of the street.

"So," he said, "you asked God about something, and you got an answer. What's the problem with that?"

She let go of his hand to grab his arm instead, and she stopped him, then tugged him to turn enough to face her. They'd traveled only a few steps from the weak bulb above the bar door, but the darkness had mostly engulfed them, and he could see only her eyes peering out from the shadows.

He snorted softly when he saw those eyes look up so that she could spin the umbrella, placing the hole, and its constant drip like a broken faucet, off to the side.

"That helps," he said.

Then, she turned her eyes back to him.

"Do you suppose you'd recognize God if he talked to you? You'd know his voice?"

"Wouldn't it be obvious?"

He grinned and hoped that she could see it.

"Maybe like a choir in the background? I bet I'd hear a harp too."

She scoffed and shook her head, and he let his grin dwindle.

"You can't be that naive. You've watched too many stupid movies."

Socrates, with no trace of a grin, stared at her. And he knew that his lips were moving, but the words hadn't caught up yet.

"With that Old Serpent running loose in the world and so good at telling lies, he could probably scam you pretty easy, right? How would you know?"

"Old . . . Old Serpent?

"Yeah, I read that somewhere. The devil. Heard of him?"

"Uh, yeah. I sometimes think he lives around here."

"Yeah. Everywhere else too."

"Uh, even in churches?"

There was just enough light for him to see her shrug.

He coughed and was about to speak when she began walking toward the street again, with Socrates pulled along behind her.

"I guess it would be pretty easy. To get scammed."

Then, mostly to himself, he said, "For someone that goes by a name like that."

Chapter 12 – I'm Trapped

They reached the street, and she took them to the left, along a wet sidewalk where shaky streetlight reflections floated past, so dim that they seemed to be drowning.

The umbrella hole above them dripped steadily, and she kept it between them and behind them.

Socrates kept trying to step between puddles and sometimes ventured a glance up at her. She caught his eye, then pointed with a tip of her head toward the awning that they were approaching, one not too different from his own.

Before they reached their shelter, she said, "Piece of shit. Just another thing to use up and toss aside."

"Huh?"

"Nothing. Just being philosophical."

She stopped long enough to throw the broken umbrella out into the street, where the gutter flow caused a steady lifting and bouncing of the fabric.

He stopped with her, and they both watched the gritty river along the curb carrying trash and gurgling what it could through a sewer grate, leaving the rest of it snagged there.

"Where does it all go, Socrates?"

"Who knows? Away from here."

He began walking, bringing her with him, and they huddled side by side out of the rain beneath the awning.

"I wasn't always a hooker, you know."

"Of course. That would be weird."

"You're funny. You know what I mean."

"So, what got you going on that?"

"Oh, shit. We're going there?"

"Only if you want to."

"I don't want to."

He held his watch higher and for more time than needed, then let his arm drop again.

"You have some free time. It's last call, remember?"

With their shoulders rubbing together, both watching the rain falling unnoticed by most on an empty avenue, she turned to see him looking at her with a faint grin.

She pointed at him and said, "You're kind of a smartass."

His grin grew into an actual smile, and he looked back out at the dark street.

"I don't know. Maybe."

She joined him in studying the lonely scene, puffed up her cheeks, then let it escape in a rush.

"Alright. I'd been out of school a while, and all I cared about was partying and meeting guys."

"You weren't asking God about anything yet, right?"

"I probably never would have. So, I got mixed up with some sick freak and like an idiot, I shot up some shit he gave me. God, I almost died."

While she drew in another breath, Socrates said, "That's when God or someone else talked to you? When you were high?"

"Shit, will you let me tell the story? Damn, Socrates."

"Sorry. Don't know when to shut it."

"No one does. Yeah, that's when that idea came to me. Maybe it was because of whatever that shit was. No way it should have been that bad."

"Sounds like you just got a bad batch."

"Must have been. He said it would be fine, the fucking liar."

He looked quickly and saw her frowning out at the night.

"So, I wasn't just high. Something about that was all messed up."

He said, "I guess weird ideas come at weird times."

"I guess so. I kind of lost my focus after that. That idea's been eating me alive ever since."

"Sorry. That doesn't sound good."

"It isn't. Anyway, I never took any drugs ever again. Am I any kind of role model, though? Hell, no. Look what I do for a living."

He turned to her and glanced down quickly before she could turn to see where he was looking.

"There are far worse things."

Up close, sheltered from the rain, she studied him with slowly blinking eyes.

"You sure? Sometimes, I think it's like some kind of blasphemy."

"Well, I don't know. You're serving a need that—"

He locked onto her staring eyes when she said, "All they want is that flash of pleasure. We should be asking how it can feel that damn good. I mean, when it's done right. Not the shit I'm doing with them."

"I, uh, we—"

"Shouldn't it be so much more than that flash, Socrates? They don't give a damn about any deeper meaning. It's all just so goddamn superficial."

He paused long enough to watch her focus on each of his eyes a couple of times. Even without much light, the wet sheen on her eyes was noticeable.

"Well, yeah, that's kind of lousy."

She leaned in even closer and held a hand near his face, her fingers showing a short gap between them. Her face curled up into a snarl.

"I'm this fucking close, Socrates. This is all wrong, the way I'm living. But I don't know what else to do."

He held her intense gaze and when he turned just his eyes to focus on her hand, she lowered it.

"Uh, I bet you could do a lot of other things. You're smart. You can figure something out."

She scoffed but continued to look into his eyes.

"In the meantime, though, you do look good. That counts."

She kept staring, her eyes still wet.

"Why, thanks."

She blinked them both, sending a thin wet streak down one of her cheeks.

"You don't," she said. "You look like shit."

He gave her a smile and said, "Well, I mostly just drink and feed the birds."

In the dim light, he saw again that smile that rarely appeared as she wiped at her cheek.

"And lean," she said, still holding his gaze. "You said you lean."

He looked from her eyes to her smile again, just for a second, then looked out from their dry refuge from the rain.

"Damn wind."

He looked back again just to return her smile, then they both looked to the left at the sound of an approaching vehicle, and they watched as another police car passed by slowly, with no lights or siren chirps.

Looking to the right, they stood close, out of the weather, and kept watching until its taillights had become tiny red dots that got choked by the gloom and damp.

*　*　*

Silence, unbroken except for the relentless tapping of rain on the awning and plinking into puddles, returned to the deserted city. He kept himself from looking but still, he smiled when he felt her hold his right arm with both hands, keeping herself pressed up against him.

"It's a cold goddamn world sometimes."

Nodding, he said, "The wind. I kind of hate the wind."

"Yeah, so you said. So, I got an answer, and I don't know what to do with it. Shit, I can't even kill myself now."

"I saw the scissors. Kind of a grisly way to go. Why would you want that? Because of some answer?"

Her grip on his arm tightened as she let out one near-hysterical laugh that got picked apart by the rain before it could bounce off of the bricks across the street.

"Yeah, Socrates, because I don't know who gave me that idea. Was it from God? Or was Lucifer the son of a bitch that shot that idea into my head?"

"Lucifer. That's kind of a cool name. He's also the Old Serpent, right?"

"Try to pay attention, will you? So, which one fed that idea to me?"

"Does it matter?"

When she turned her face toward him, he noticed and turned his too.

"Hell, yeah, it matters. If God told me that idea, he'd want me to share it with the world, right? But what if it's Lucifer's idea, and he wants me to share it? I should keep my goddamn mouth shut, then."

"Fine, so just keep it to yourself."

He looked from one wide open eye to the other and back again.

"You don't get it," she said. "Maybe God singled me out to tell everyone?"

"Oh, I get it. I think. God picked a hooker for the big reveal?"

He watched her eyes narrow into tight slits as she shook her head at him.

"Is that all I am?"

"Oh, um, no. I didn't mean—"

"Forget it. It's a touchy subject sometimes."

He watched her watching him back and couldn't find any words quickly enough.

"Um . . ."

She smiled and saved him.

"That was meant to be funny. Hooker. Touchy. Go ahead and laugh."

He laughed once and looked out into the rain.

"Yeah, that's pretty good."

"Anyway," she said, "it's like I have God whispering in one ear and Satan in the other. Like they're both sitting on my shoulders. Well, dammit, does one of them carry more weight? Which one—"

"What? On both of your shoulders? That's what does it? So, you're probably leaning, too, because one's a lot heavier, and—"

"I'm not leaning anywhere. I'm trapped. That's what I am."

Socrates looked down, first to the right, then the left, and saw that he was leaning. He picked up his left hand to check those fingernails, and she grabbed his right hand.

"Come on. I'll show you something. You in the mood for some show and tell?"

He leaned out quickly and glanced down at her legs, which were picking up what little light was out there with them.

"Not that, perv. Something else."

He straightened up and smiled, looking into her eyes again.

"Damn, they're pretty nice."

He saw nothing but her smile when she said, "Thanks. Aren't they, though?"

Chapter 13 – His Expressionless Face

His hand in hers, both wet from misty rain without even a broken umbrella for help, she towed him along. He sometimes focused on her hair, some of which had twisted itself into the matted fur of her jacket, and dared, when he could, to glance down at her legs, which were long, on display, and stabbing her heels into the sidewalk confidently.

He looked up when she leaned her head enough to call to him over her shoulder, almost laughing out the words.

"You just need to see it."

He ran a few quick steps to get even with her, but she only looked ahead, walking with determination. With only a straight walkway ahead of them, at least for a short while, he rushed a look at his right hand's fingernails.

He'd fallen behind her again while holding his hand closer, checking the lengths and trying to remember how long they were on the left hand.

"You said you feel them on your shoulders? And one's heavier?"

"Just keep up. Forget that—I was only talking."

He dropped his right hand and hurried again until he was beside her, and she almost immediately brought them both to a stop just before they would have stepped into the mouth of another alley.

It was dark, too dark for him to see anything, so he looked at her instead. While she stared intently, her eyes moving slowly and scanning it well, he studied her unblemished skin, the graceful lines of her cheek, and the length of her eyelashes as she blinked slowly.

He'd just begun an admiring review of her lips when they began curling into a relieved smile.

"Perfect. This'll do."

"Um, you really see something?"

"Yeah. Of course."

She jerked his arm as she lunged into the night, her heels sounding on the wet pavement as she pulled him in after her.

He was straining to see where the puddles were and weren't when he heard her say, "Satan probably put that there."

"Huh? Lucifer, you mean?"

She laughed just once, then said, over her shoulder, "Same guy, I think. Hell if I know. Anyway, maybe God put it there."

*　*　*

He walked even with her, matching her steps, but tipped his head each way to try to see what she saw. All he saw was a bunch of night trapped between dark walls that he guessed were brick.

Miley slowed, and he slowed with her and when she looked up, he did too. She'd led them underneath a complicated metal structure not too high above the pavement, and he noticed its crisscrossing metal pieces somehow blacker than the black night sky looking in on them between the buildings.

After snapping her hand away from his, she jumped, doing her best in high heels and a skirt, but she'd never come close.

"Grab that," she said.

He was still looking down at her legs, illuminated in some way, attracting what few traces of light had ventured in that far. She saw him and waved her hand in front of his face, so close that she almost slapped him.

"Hey. Forget the hooker's legs for a second."

Using the hand still in front of his face, she pointed up, causing him to look up too.

"Up there. The fire escape."

"Um, I probably shouldn't go to your place. I thought you said—"

"What? No, I, uh, don't live here. You really think I'm taking you home? Just get that ladder down, alright?"

"Sure."

He easily jumped up and grabbed the lowest bar, then hung there and let his weight pull the narrow ladder down until it hit the ground. Before he could comment, she bumped him aside with her hip and started to climb, so he grabbed it to help hold it steady.

After she'd climbed a few rungs, her thighs were about even with his eyes, and he made no effort to stop looking or even back away. And when she continued up, he watched her the entire way.

Even when he fished out the whiskey bottle, uncapped it, and took a couple of generous drinks, he kept his eyes riveted on the sight of her legs, which were about the only things visible.

She stopped on the landing two stories up. He held the bottle, still in his coat pocket, and began drawing it out again. But he let it drop back in at the sight of her tipping herself out, holding the rail around the small landing.

"What the hell are you doing?"

In the meager light, past her legs, he could see her face, and he watched as she looked first one way along the alley—from where they came—then the other way—toward another quiet street in the distance.

Still looking each way and not down, she said, "Look. What do you see?"

"I looked. Nothing. Why?"

Despite the steady plinking of raindrops in puddles and on the wet alley floor, he heard her scoff.

"Keep watching."

He looked up for a while, then looked one way along the alley, then the other way. Looking back up, he stepped away to get a better view of her climbing up onto the lowest cross bar of the railing.

She'd gotten one shoe up, and he said, "Hey. Careful. I wouldn't want you to fall off of there."

She only laughed, looked each way, then stepped up her other shoe. She straightened herself up, her heels both hooked on it, then she looked each way.

"Hey," he said, "that's not a good—"

"There," she said, pointing toward the far end of the alley. "See it?"

Socrates looked and far away, as far as that next street, almost lost in the mist and light rain, stood a figure. It wore a hat with a wide brim, and its long coat twitched sporadically with the breezes.

The faint streetlights behind the figure rendered it nothing more than a silhouette.

"That guy?" said Socrates. "He's probably wondering what you're—"

"You still don't get it. Watch."

He looked up and held his breath at the sight of her stepping up onto the next rail, the middle one, leaving the very top one to press into her shins.

She extended her arms out over the alley below, swung her arms around when she almost fell, then pointed toward the figure.

Socrates snapped his head that way and watched it hurrying toward them, taking strong steps, sometimes splashing heavily as it drew near.

"Well, he thinks you're going to—"

When she laughed, in a mirthless way, he looked up at her.

"Damn right, it does. Well, there's no way the damn thing will let me splatter myself down there."

Before answering her, Socrates turned to again look at the approaching stranger, and he barely caught himself from stumbling backwards at seeing him standing next to him, so close that he could have knocked the hat loose.

That figure was also leaning back, the hat brim tipped up at Miley.

With only traces of light deep in that alley, but with eyes that had adjusted to it, Socrates could see that their guest didn't wear just that wide-brimmed hat. He also wore dark sunglasses. And what appeared to be a priest's collar. And his expressionless face displayed a large "X" tattooed directly beneath his left eye, positioned low enough to not be blocked by the glasses.

"Who are—"

He looked up at hearing Miley's loud laughter.

"Fine," said Miley. "I'm done for now. Go back wherever the hell you came from."

Socrates watched her start climbing back down, then turned to address the stranger, but he was gone. He hadn't made a sound and besides the sounds of Miley's heels on metal and an occasional cuss word, the alley again offered only muted rain sounds.

He looked back up, seeing again that her legs were the most visible of all things in the darkness.

"Who was that? You know him?"

He heard a low howling, odd in its tone, advertising neither fear, nor aggression, nor any recognizable sentiment.

He spun as quickly as he could, ending its call, and he held himself still, looking around in the dark. There was only rainfall in the night.

Just about to step down to the alley, Miley said, "It wasn't a—"

His words hissed out hushed and panicked at the same time.

"Did you hear that?"

She scoffed and said, "Not a damn thing. Never do. I'm just trying not to twist an ankle. That thing probably wouldn't care about that."

He watched one way, then quickly turned to look the other way. He was about to continue when she stood close to him, wiping her hands.

She laughed dryly and said, "I'd probably have to offer a discount. A damaged goods sale, you know, and—"

"You really didn't hear anything?"

"That thing is always quiet like that. Did you see how quick it showed up to stop me from jumping?"

"What? He had a collar. I think that was a priest. He probably—"

"Oh, a priest. Right. Whatever, it wouldn't have let me kill myself. You saw that much, at least, right?"

"I, um, I think I saw a priest that tried to—"

"Damn. Obviously, we're not done yet."

"But he—"

He stopped at seeing her tip her head and squint at him. Then, she grabbed his hand and began leading him back out to the street and spoke while he tried catching up with her.

"You need more proof. Fine. It even took me a while to believe this shit was happening."

He jerked her hard enough to stop her in her tracks at the sound of an animal wailing in pain behind him.

He didn't turn to look but said to her, "Okay, but you . . . you had to have heard—"

"Try to focus, alright? God, you're all over the place."

She tipped her head toward the street, he didn't move, then she began dragging him along. He glanced once behind himself, then hurried to walk beside her.

*   *   *

She led him in silence out of the alley, and they began a journey next to the empty street, puddles instead of people all around them.

Keeping up with her, looking at her when he could, he said, "Where are we going?"

"A place where I can show you how that thing won't let me die. You're not convinced."

He laughed just once, a strained laugh, and gave a quick glance behind them.

"Thing? It was just a priest."

She stopped them both and glared at him.

"It wasn't a goddamn priest."

"Sure looked like a priest."

She scoffed and shook her head, ready to snarl again at him.

Behind him, something screeched, the volume starting low and increasing, reaching a panicked level. Like it was sprinting in to attack him, but it quieted itself instead.

He winced, watching her, and saw that she'd had no reaction.

"You really didn't . . . you, um—"

"No. I only thought it was a priest the first time. It's not, Socrates. No way."

He stared at her as she waited for him to speak. It took a moment.

"No. I mean, did you hear . . ."

She just kept staring, tipping her head.

"Never mind."

Chapter 14 – A Lunatic Streetwalker

Miley held his hand, and he kept up with her as they walked in light rainfall along the street in a city that hadn't yet awakened. He saw that they were approaching another alley on his right side, an opening that looked like a tall door to nothing but darkness.

"Where are you taking me?"

"Damn," she said, "I wouldn't believe me either. I'll have to put on a real goddamn show for you."

They were just about to pass the alley, which was darker than the last one.

"What kind of—"

From far back in the depths, insane cackling erupted, almost like laughter, the kind a hyena might scream out before, during, or after a meaty kill. He jerked her to a stop and stared in, shaking his head and seeing nothing but night.

"What now?"

"There's . . . there's something in there. You didn't hear it?"

She scoffed and got a better grip on his hand, then tipped her head toward where she was leading him.

"Don't start losing it on me, Socrates. God, you're a distracting kind of guy."

* * *

As Miley dragged him along, taking strong strides and holding his hand, the rain increased. The low clouds suffocated the city, and the widely-spaced streetlights didn't possess enough ambition to put up a fight.

He'd just looked up from watching his right foot achieve a nearly symmetrical splash and saw that she'd turned enough that he could see her face.

"This is crazy," he said. "That was a priest back there. Of course, he'd try to stop you."

"Right. Last time I tried that, the damn thing caught me."

"From a jump? No way. You must know that sounds crazy."

She stopped to bend over for a piece of cardboard leaning against the bricks, and he didn't notice it, or the wall, or the rain, or anything but her legs.

He snapped his eyes back up when she began dragging him a few more steps toward a bench. She bumped a hip into him, forcing him to sit, and she sat close beside him.

While holding the flimsy shield above them both, she said, "I know it's crazy, but you just don't get it. It's from that idea. You'll understand when I tell you. If you're nuts enough to still want me to."

He saw that she was staring straight out, shaking her head slowly.

"I, um, maybe I—"

"Yeah. You should just run. Are you going to bail on this, Socrates? Or do you want in on this little nightmare of mine?"

He tipped only his eyes down toward her legs, her thighs wet from the rain and her knees propped up by heels on the sidewalk. When he finally looked up again, it was to see that she'd been watching him at least part of that time.

She grinned and said, "You got a thing for hookers, don't you? That's the only reason you're even considering it."

"What? I mean, you look—"

"Hey, I'm not judging. That's your business. So, do you want to know or not? You're already out in the rain when sane people should be home in bed."

"Sure. I want to know. Tell me."

"First, you tell me why you like hookers. Because it doesn't make any sense to me why anyone would."

He looked down and off to the right, away from her legs.

"Wow. No one's ever asked me that."

"Well, I'm asking."

"Alright. I think it's because I don't ever have to know if they care about me or not. I'd never even ask."

At the sound of loud, agitated hooting in the branches above them, almost drowning out Miley, he grimaced and forced his eyes to look only straight ahead.

"That's some interesting philosophical bullshit you've thrown together. Okay, then. Let's just—"

"Wait. You didn't hear that either?"

He stabbed a finger toward the trees above. She looked up for a second, then shook her head and looked back at him.

"Hear what? What are you talking about?"

"Something. Never mind. I don't know."

"I wasn't really going to jump off that fire escape, and it still showed up. Watch what happens when I really want to jump."

He watched her chest rise with a sigh, then she wiped once under each eye, still looking forward.

"You, um, you really want to?"

"Hell yeah, but it doesn't matter. I'm protected by a goddamn freak."

* * *

"This really isn't working," she said, tipping her head up toward the cardboard she was holding over them.

"Yeah. It's pretty shitty."

"It'll have to do. You ready to move?"

"Yeah. Oh, wait."

He watched her turn toward him, and he looked only at her growing smile as he reached up, removed his hat, and held it out over her lap.

Her smile grew even more, and he looked into her eyes when he said, "Sorry. I can't believe I'm just now thinking of that."

She never broke their gaze as she took his fedora and placed it lightly on her head like a crown. Still smiling, she wiped under her eyes, once each side.

"No. This is a perfect time," she said and let the cardboard fall behind them. "You going to be okay?"

"Sure. I'll be fine."

She turned her eyes up toward the brim and said, "How's it look?"

He laughed and said, "Way better on you."

Looking into his eyes again, as they sat close on a park bench in the early morning hours, she said, "Well, I'm a professional."

They both laughed while he said, "Yep. Yeah. A philosopher too."

She nodded, then looked away after a few seconds, coughed lightly into her hand, and stood up. He found the resolve to not look at her bare legs so close to his eyes.

"So," she said, "let's just get going. Come on."

She took his hand, helped him up, and he joined her to continue their walk along the deserted city sidewalk.

"You should be able to ask God for answers, right?" he said. "Isn't that a basic Bible thing?"

"Who knows? Depends on who wrote it."

"Huh? It's supposed to be the Word of God, right? You don't think so?"

"Was anyone there to see it written? Anyone alive now?"

"So, it's not from God, then, like they tell us?"

"Shit, it's naive to even believe that it is anymore. Is there anything in this world that hasn't been corrupted?"

He hesitated for a moment, focusing on trying to miss most of the puddles.

"I never thought about it. Probably not."

She scoffed and shook her head a few times.

"It would have been so easy to change some words over the centuries. Or all of them. Or maybe people just added shit. Why would anyone think that hasn't been fucked around with too?"

"Either way, what's wrong with asking for answers? Isn't that—"

A single loud roar, like from a lion, came from so close behind him that he shivered and snapped his head around, but he didn't slow his pace.

Nothing was there, so he looked to Miley.

"You had to hear that. You had to."

"Only the rain, Socrates. Don't lose your mind out here, alright?"

*   *   *

They'd just reached an intersection, and Miley looked to their right, then took him with her to cross. Halfway there, she stopped and Socrates didn't let go of her hand, so he stopped with her.

"What are you doing?" he said.

"I don't know. Waiting for a truck? A big one."

He yanked her arm hard enough to shake her, causing her to snort a single laugh until they'd reached the far sidewalk.

She stopped him there and laughed again.

"I kind of feel better already. I never talk to anyone about all of this crap."

"There's more? What other crap?"

"Oh, shit. You should see all I've written down about this."

"A diary?"

"Yeah," she said, looking into his eyes. "I'll call it 'The Diary of a Lunatic Streetwalker.'"

He grinned and said, "There's more than one?"

Squinting, she said, "God, you're a smartass. Fine. '*The* Lunatic Streetwalker.'"

He looked ahead along the sidewalk, she watched him for a moment, then sighed and started walking with him.

"No comment about that title?"

"Oh," he said, "I was just, um, thinking that walking is pretty healthy."

She laughed, still looking ahead, and said, "You're really zeroing in on the one positive thing about that. Decent of you."

"I try. Sometimes. No, really, what other crap?"

"Okay, you asked for it. Here's something that's been making me nuts. It's all mixed up in my head all the time."

"Even when you're, um, you know. Working?"

"Especially then—I'm so fucking far away you wouldn't believe it. You've heard of the Lord's Prayer, right?"

"Well, yeah. Everyone has."

"Do you ever say it? I mean, really say that out loud to pray?"

"I have. Sure. Why?"

"Alone?"

"Yeah. Always alone, I guess."

"Do you feel stupid saying '*Our* Father' and 'Give *us* this day?'"

"Uh, no. That's the prayer."

She tipped her head back, cackling, but the brim of his hat kept the rain off of her face. But he caught a quick glimpse of wet drops still resting on the soft skin of her cheek.

"You're alone, and you're saying 'we' and 'us?' That's not stupid? God's supposed to take you seriously? You must sound like a disrespectful idiot to him."

"I don't know. What's your point?"

She snapped his hand down, stopping him with her as she faced him.

"Something fucked with that prayer, too, Socrates. Made a mockery of it. Turned it into an irritating joke that everyone blabs right in God's face."

She'd already started them again, not waiting for an answer, and they were approaching the next street.

Behind him, above the sound of rain hitting the concrete, he heard grunting, yapping, and flapping wings. It sounded like just one, then a few, then many.

They were angry, hungry, and so close that they were about to—

Socrates snapped his head around.

But he saw nothing. No attacking birds. Only rain.

"But Miley, it's just a prayer. That's not such a big—"

"Change the words, Socrates. Goddammit, say, 'My Father.' Say, 'Give me this day.' And all the rest. More personal that way? Just you talking to God, like probably how you're supposed to?"

"I, um, I guess. I mean, it's just—"

"Do you ever talk to anyone like that? Like you're somehow a goddamn bunch of people?"

He didn't answer, and she let the question hang there as they plodded on a few more steps.

"Of course, you don't. No sane person does. If they did, you'd run from them. You know what else?"

"Uh, what?"

"If you're acting like there's a bunch of people around you and there aren't, isn't that lying? You're lying to God in a prayer?"

"Wow. That's kind of—"

"It's kind of fucking wrong. Yeah."

A few more quiet steps later, she said, "Speaking of running, there's no way I'm about to. Let's take a cab."

"Where to?"

"A bridge."

"There's one two blocks from here."

"Not high enough. I want to have time while I'm falling to properly cuss out all this bullshit."

"Until the priest catches you, you mean?"

She stopped him, and they turned toward each other, huddled alone on the rainy city sidewalk.

Miley smiled and pointed at him.

"About time. You're catching on, Socrates. Except it isn't no goddamn priest. Angel? Demon? Who the fuck knows?"

Chapter 15 – Stop the Goddamn Cab

Socrates pointed toward the left, and they both watched a vehicle approaching, its headlights doing little more than giving it two glowing damp clouds to chase.

"Think it's a cab?"

Miley said, "We'll find out."

They were both standing by the curb, and she reached out and up, stretching, and he didn't fight his eyes dropping back down to the sight of her legs.

"I think it's a cab," she said, then quickly turned back to him.

He looked away from her legs, not quite quickly enough, and said, "Oh, yeah, let's hope so."

She resumed her summoning of it, saying over her shoulder, "We could walk, but I just thought of something: we get that cab up to some crazy speed, then I'll jerk the steering wheel, maybe roll the damn thing. No way that freak could catch a goddamn rolling car."

"What? No way. I'm not suicidal."

"You will be if you ride my story to its end. You'll be begging to get ripped open in a rolling cab."

"You sure have a way with words. Uh, I'm not exactly in the mood for a cab ride."

She relaxed at seeing for sure that it was a cab and stood beside him.

"Really? It's the whole rolling over thing, isn't it?"

He didn't laugh when he said, "More the ripping open thing. Doesn't sound like fun."

"Maybe that thing'll catch your ass too. Take a goddamn chance, Socrates."

"You're really going to crash it?"

She left his question floating out in the rain as the cab pulled along the curb. She opened the back door, sat herself inside, and started shimmying over, grinning up at him while she gestured with one curling finger for him to join her.

"Take a ride with the hooker."

He looked both ways, then scoffed and got in and clunked the door shut after him.

* * *

He found that Miley had moved over only to the middle of the backseat, and he pushed in close, feeling her warm up against him. She held his hat close to the floormat on her side and shook it, then put it back on.

She gave him a quick smile, he returned it with a shrug, then they both looked forward.

The cab driver kept looking straight ahead, and Miley said, "To the bridge, ten blocks straight ahead."

The driver nodded, his dark ball cap tipping, but he didn't speak. He only put the car in gear and with the engine revving modestly, he pulled them away from the curb.

Miley elbowed Socrates, then said, "And make it fast. Get this piece of shit moving, alright?"

From the backseat, they both watched and saw not a single reaction from the driver. No head tipping to acknowledge her demand. No change of speed. No words spoken.

Miley leaned forward, trying to tip her head enough to see his face. She leaned back and only squinted at Socrates.

He shrugged, then scooted himself forward and tried to see the cabbie's face too. He shook his head at not having any success, then he looked down on the front seat.

76

He turned back toward Miley, his eyes wide open, and tipped his head toward the seat.

She leaned forward and looked for herself, then she sat back quickly. He joined her.

She leaned close to his ear and whispered, "How did it get a cab?"

He shook his head, and she turned enough that he could whisper to her, "More than that: how did he *know* to get a cab?"

She scowled at him, then sat back, rigid and staring straight ahead. She still spoke softly to Socrates.

"God. Get me the fuck out of here."

Then, she caused Socrates to shrink back when she screamed, "This is far enough! Stop the goddamn cab!"

The driver again offered no reaction. He remained silent, facing away from his passengers, and kept the car at a steady pace.

"Goddammit," she said, then she reached over Socrates for the door handle, popped it enough to cause the interior lights to switch on, and turned to direct her next scream directly at the driver.

"I'll jump! You're not that goddamn quick. Stop the fucking car!"

The car slowed, but without any urgency, and pulled along the curb. Miley began shoving on Socrates with her elbow and kicking him with her knee, forcing him out and onto the sidewalk. She stood beside him and slammed the door.

They watched the cab roll away at a leisurely pace, and they kept staring until it had been mostly digested by the rain-clogged air in the distance.

"Holy fuck! Socrates, what the fuck?"

"I know. He didn't even charge you."

"Not that! Goddammit, Socrates!"

"Sorry. How does a priest get a—"

"Oh, shit. It wasn't a goddamn priest. I saw its fucking hat, right there on the seat. That freak put on a goddamn ball cap, then stole a cab?"

"We'll never know which one came first. If it were me, I might have—"

She shoved him back a step with both hands.

"It doesn't matter! Dammit, you don't know when to stop!"

"Sorry again. Hey, wait a second. Isn't riding in that cab about the safest place for you?"

"That's a shitty suggestion, dammit. That thing scares the shit out of me."

She paused for a moment, then said, "So . . . could you tell?

"Tell what?"

"Which goddamn side it's playing for?"

Looking into her eyes, he took just enough time to puff up his cheeks, then let it seep out slowly.

"No. Sorry."

She shook her head, then looked in the direction of the cab.

"You can still see him out there," she said, "driving that thing, and we're close to that bridge. We can get there quick, and that son of a bitch will be miles away."

She began a quick walk, and he rushed to catch up, saying, "Right. Yeah. Because that would make sense. Like the rest of it."

Chapter 16 – I'm Your Father?

Before Miley pointed at it, Socrates had seen ahead of them the low structure seeming to grow up from the asphalt roadway. The street beside them continued through between its side railings, rising up, then looking like it had been chopped off where it settled back to street level on the hidden other side.

A single car had just crested the bridge's high point, traveling toward them. Two cylinders of light pointed up into the mist, then lowered to reflect off of the wet pavement.

On each side of the bridge, nearly black gouges stretched out in each direction, a gorge that separated their side from the other side. Beyond that dark valley, a city street advertised the day's beginning with a patchy parade of headlights and taillights crawling both ways.

"There's the bridge," she said, pointing ahead. "Told you it was close."

"You're not seriously planning what I think you're planning, are you?"

In a weary voice, she said, "Oh, Socrates, it won't let me die."

"That priest?"

He gave her a moment to correct him, but she didn't, then he grinned and said, "Besides, he drove away."

She scoffed and said, "Right. That priest. Try talking to it. Call it 'Father.' See how that works out."

She spat out the comment then started hiking toward the bridge. Before she could get too far, he reached for her hand and hurried to walk beside her.

"Fine. I will. What's wrong with calling him that?"

"Isn't God the father? Who said you should call some common guy, someone that learned to recite stuff by an altar and wears funny clothes, 'Father?'"

"Let me guess: Lucifer?"

"Hey," she said, "it's his world. Might be just another way of sticking it to God. Just a fun little way to piss him off."

She stopped them both before one more step would put them on the bridge. The oncoming vehicle was rolling by, and Socrates watched the curious driver give them a long stare as she passed. He checked Miley's face and found that she'd been looking only straight ahead.

"Changing your mind?"

"No. Suicide's just not much fun. Yeah, you were right: probably Lucifer."

He slipped the bottle out of his coat pocket, checked the quantity, then held it out front for her to see, shaking it to get it sloshing around inside.

"Here. This helps keep me balanced."

"Getting drunk? Really?"

"Well, more just the weight of it. It's hard to explain."

She accepted it, one hand around its neck, but didn't thank him. She unscrewed the cap, tipped it back for a few swallows, then recapped it.

"That's not bad. Okay, start seeing the world, Socrates, as corrupted in every way you can imagine."

"So, more than what you've said already?"

"Way more. Come on."

She grabbed his hand and tugged on it, but he didn't budge. She looked back and saw him holding out his free hand.

"I need that back. Uh, if you're done."

She laughed and held it back with one hand, like she was about to throw it.

"Bullshit. 'The weight of it.' Shit, the things people tell themselves."

He stared at the bottle, cocked and ready to fly, and said, smiling, "Hey, maybe this is a better plan: how about if I throw you off the bridge?"

She snorted out a single laugh, then said, "That's it. Get that brain working on something creative."

"Alright. Try this: I'd be playing catch with that priest, right?"

Miley only stared for a second, then scoffed at him.

"Yeah. That's actually kind of funny. You'd probably want the bottle back first, though, right?"

"Well, yeah."

She opened it for another chug, then capped it and handed it to him. He drank some, too, before stuffing it back into his pocket.

She watched until the bottle was out of sight, then said, "Are we finally fucking ready?"

"Sure. Just remember that that priest is miles away by now."

She tipped her head back to laugh, then began dragging him along with her onto the bridge.

"Well, we'll fucking see."

*　*　*

They trod out onto the bridge, him along the rail and her holding his hand. She kept focusing ahead as he maneuvered her closer to the rail so that he could look over. He heard another car passing them, going in their direction, but he didn't turn to look.

Over the rail, he saw that they'd begun traveling out over the dark abyss that he'd seen from a distance. The ground below was dropping steeply toward a single pair of train tracks far below. A line of lampposts, some missing, some leaning, and none of them lit, kept the rails company.

"Here's not high enough for you?" he said.

"I'd rather boost the drama, alright?"

"I'd rather you don't. You want the highest spot?"

"Yeah, but hold up a second."

81

She stopped and slipped her hand away from his, then stretched her arms out to her sides, drawing in a deep breath. She let it out slowly while watching a single vehicle passing them in each direction. The sky in the distance showed just a hint of day creeping up above the horizon.

"Shit," she said, "I feel better already just from telling you stuff. Here's some more of my philosophizing. Forget that so-called Lord's Prayer for a second. Do you ever pray and ask God for things?"

"Yeah, when I pray. If, I mean. That's the point, right?"

"I don't think so. That's been screwed up too. Do you know better than God, Socrates, about anything? You're that smart?"

"Uh, no. Not even close."

"But you're going to tell him what to give you? You somehow, some way know what's best for you?"

He exhaled deeply before answering.

"Wow. No. Oh, how about this: what if I pray for good health? Something simple like that. Pretty reasonable, right?"

She was still looking for a sunrise, shaking her head slowly.

"Well, that does seem reasonable, but it's probably not that easy. Maybe you need to be sick for part of a bigger plan. That could be, right?"

"I guess. Sure. So, why bother praying, then? Is that what you mean?"

"No, that's not what I mean. I think we should pray only to have enough faith, and maybe strength, to accept whatever God has planned for us. That's it. That's all."

"Like him dumping that idea on you, the one you want to kill yourself over? That's what God has planned for you? How's that working out?"

She turned to him and let out a deep sigh, then looked from one of his eyes to the other and back.

"It's not working out. And maybe it's not from God, remember? Anyway, it's show time."

She reclaimed his hand and together, they walked out toward the high point of the bridge, where she'd have the highest fall.

* * *

She looked all around, then herded him over to the rail and let go of his hand. He stayed where she'd put him and watched her continue to study the scene. She paced one way, then the other, sometimes looking along the roadway, sometimes out beyond the rail.

He stayed quiet, sometimes looking toward the increasing traffic navigating the road crossing on the other side, until she'd placed herself at the rail several steps away from him, facing out. He walked over and pressed his left side into her, and they both held the rail.

"Think you got it?"

"The highest point?" she said. "Yeah, I think so."

"Right in the middle," he said. "I like that. That's good too."

"Glad you're happy."

"I'm not. Anyway, it's all about the same. I think you're stalling."

She looked at his eyes, up close, and said, "A smartass to the end."

He waited until she'd resumed scanning the horizon, then said, "Maybe I just want to see you smile."

He watched her continue to stare out along the tracks without any reaction for a second or two. Just before he was about to give up, she turned to him, held his gaze, and gave him a brief smile, then looked away again. He smiled and looked away too.

They both watched the sliver of lighter sky clinging to the horizon off where the tracks had shrunk together into a point and silhouettes of buildings formed a low, jagged handsaw's edge.

The streetlights up on the bridge had switched off, and they stood in near darkness. From their place high on the bridge, the other side's streams of cars and trucks sent them a low rumble.

"All those things I just vomited up to you, all about—"

"The Bible, priests, prayers, and—"

"Yeah, all of that. They're all crosswinds, Socrates. Long-range shooting, remember? It takes only—"

"A small wind, yeah. To get you off target. You're finally getting back to shooting talk?"

She turned to scoff at him.

"You're kind of an impatient SOB, you know that?"

He turned to her and shrugged.

"Yeah, sometimes, I guess. But hey, this stuff doesn't happen to me every day. Okay, so, what's the deal with the shooting and winds?"

She looked again toward the rising sun.

"So, tell me: what do you suppose is the biggest fucked-up thing of all?"

She turned back to him, and he again saw a soft sheen on her eyes as she waited for his response.

"Those are all pretty damn big. You're saying the devil messed up all of that?"

She blinked a few times and looked beyond the railing again.

"Maybe. How could anyone know? But those are puny compared to the one that I wish I'd never thought of."

"Maybe you didn't think of it. You said the idea came to you, right? One on each shoulder? But one is heavier than—"

She spun to face him again.

"That doesn't matter. Forget about things on your shoulders, alright? Dammit, Socrates."

He spoke while turning away from her direct stare.

"Sure. Jesus."

She shook her head just once, smirked, and looked away from him and toward the slice of brighter sky.

"That's funny, and you don't even know why. Maybe I've told you enough. Do you want to be damned too? Really, you're better off not knowing anything."

She turned toward him and waited until a single loud truck had passed behind them, then, when she saw that he was looking into her eyes, she said, "Not a goddamn thing."

* * *

He let a few quiet moments pass, sometimes watching her, waiting for the obvious anger and frustration to fade, but it didn't.

"You're making sense about all of that. Except for that priest. I saw his collar. He—"

"Has a weird tattoo? Really, Socrates, on his face? What priest does that? Is that standard procedure from those jokers at the Vatican?"

He leaned out over the rail, trying to keep eye contact as she leaned over to look down.

"Okay, maybe it's just some freak dressed up like—"

She scoffed loudly, and he watched her begin shaking her head.

"Yeah. And it just happens to show up at times like this."

He looked down, too, and they both saw the figure dressed like a priest directly below them, looking up.

Not moving. Not waving. Not calling out.

Just quiet and looking up.

"What the hell? He's fast. How did he—"

She scoffed again and said, "Damn fast at dumping cabs and hustling to get under a bridge."

"How the hell can he do that?"

"Because he's a goddamn freak. Maybe I can be faster, though."

She started placing one shoe on the lowest rail, then paused to watch another car pass before she continued.

"God will just have to understand the shit I'm going through."

"Oh, Miley, uh, I'm not sure that—"

"Dammit, I'm jumping," she said, looking past the railing.

Then, she turned to him and said, "Want to learn to fly with a hooker, Socrates?"

85

"I, um, I don't think—"

She laughed once and said, "Don't even think about it. You have no reason to kill yourself."

Suddenly serious, she said, "This is better. I'll die before I can tell you."

"About that idea of yours?"

"Yeah, that. Here."

He took his hat from her hand when she held it down to him, then he tried grabbing her wrist with his other hand.

"Uh, thanks. But Miley, you—"

"Don't," she said as she evaded his grasp. "This isn't your mess, Socrates."

He gave up on grabbing her, and she lifted up her other leg to stand on the lowest rail, then stood up straight, looking out toward the sunrise. She'd just begun to step one of her heels onto the next bar higher, and Socrates got shoved violently away from her, and he stumbled back and almost fell.

The priest figure was there beside Miley, still wearing his hat but not his coat. He grabbed her arm, his reach causing the loose sleeve of his robe to fall away, revealing a muscular arm covered in tattoos.

He forced her down roughly until she was standing on the wet pavement, then he released her arm. Miley teetered, fighting to keep her balance on her heels, and she stared at him, her eyes as wide as she could stretch them.

Without even a glance at Socrates, she turned and began a choppy run from them, toward the bridge's far side. To the sound of her heels poking into the concrete, Socrates turned toward the figure, who had remained standing quite near.

Another vehicle passed, aiming for the far side, and Socrates ignored it.

He took in the priest's dark glasses and a face that offered no expression at all. Just an "X" below his left eye.

He noticed that the figure's coat was lying on the ground behind him, but the priest, or so he appeared with the white collar, said nothing.

"You saved her again," said Socrates.

There was no sign that he'd even been heard.

He squinted, looking toward the dark glasses, and said, "Father."

They both stayed silent, standing close, as Miley's heels kept apprising them of her progress in fleeing the scene.

The priest tipped his head only a small amount and said, "I'm your father?"

Socrates began one slow step backwards, and the priest offered him a grin that could have been nothing more than a twitch from a raindrop clinging to his skin and trickling down to wet his upper lip.

Then, he tipped his head and hat toward Miley.

Socrates stared for less than a second before he spun around and began to race after her.

He'd taken only a few steps before he turned his head, pointing his eyes back to see the figure behind him.

But there was no one behind him.

And no coat on the slick bridge surface.

Only a quiet rainfall and the headlights of an approaching car.

He'd just turned back toward Miley and picked up his pace when he heard frantic howling and scratching from somewhere over the bridge's railing, a sound like a desperate wild animal fighting for its life to avoid falling to the tracks below.

He came to an abrupt stop, staring toward the mad beast just out of sight.

He stepped closer and put his hands on the top rail.

The howling increased, as did the scraping and clawing. The motor revving behind him couldn't block it out.

With his own low wail, he released the railing and resumed his run toward Miley.

Behind him, the sounds of howling and scratching continued but faded as he stomped toward the hooker who'd gotten a head start running from it all.

Chapter 17 – Boom, It's Right There

Running much more quickly than Miley could, dressed the way she was, Socrates closed the distance rapidly. He slowed when he heard the same wild screaming and scratching up ahead, something fighting for its life over the edge, and he stopped completely at the sight of Miley running past it and paying it no attention.

He resumed a slow run, and the frantic sounds from over the side increased as he neared their location. Just before he got there, he veered out toward the roadway's centerline, his eyes on the railing the entire time.

He never heard the truck coming up behind him, but the horn rattled him and sent him back toward the railing, where he continued sprinting after Miley.

Past that site, hearing it fading behind him, he slowed his last few steps and was able to grab her arm.

"Hey, hold up!"

She pulled herself free and kept running, and he didn't try to restrain her again. He only ran beside her and ahead of them, they saw the cross street that had increasing traffic whizzing past as the sunlight, still filtered by swollen clouds, began to render the city a lighter shade of gray.

* * *

She stopped abruptly, and he watched her place one step, then the other, past the joint marking the transition from bridge surface to a short length of road, with its own sidewalk, that led to the cross street.

"Good, you're off the bridge," he said. "Nowhere to jump."

Her only reaction was to start walking.

He took her arm again and stood beside her, stopping her, and he watched her relax with a deep sigh. She didn't try to free herself from his grip.

"Wait," he said. "Hold on a second."

With his free hand, he tipped up the back of his hat, sending it spinning off of his head, and he reached around quickly and caught it. He'd watched her the entire time, and she'd never looked over.

"I've been practicing that. I could do it again if you want."

She turned some but not enough to see him, then looked straight ahead, taking slow deep breaths.

Still holding her arm, he reached the hat over and held it in front of her. With both arms, she hugged his hat, still in his hand, and pulled it into her.

She closed her eyes and squeezed it tighter.

It could have been a single sob or maybe a deep sigh, he didn't know.

A long moment later, he said, "Um, it's still raining some. The hat might help."

She took it from his hand and placed it on her head, then, with both hands, she zipped around the brim, sending drops out from it.

"You were really going to jump?" he said.

She only looked out at the cross traffic, some of the vehicles speeding by.

"Like it would matter. You see how quick that thing is? It was at the bottom then boom, it's right there. How the fuck?"

"Uh, yeah. That's pretty damn quick."

He gave her a look and added, "Changed hats too."

She looked back at him with a squint, long enough only to shake her head a few times. He shrugged, and she resumed her study of the street ahead of them.

"Just trying to help."

She ignored him and said, "There's no way I can kill myself. Not with something like that around."

She gently worked her arm free, and he didn't fight her. Watching her legs and swaying hips as she walked away on the sidewalk, he shook his head, focused higher up, and began a quick walk after her.

"So, what's the big target that you keep talking about with all the shooting and crosswinds? Really, Miley, what the hell are you talking about?"

She stopped, and he paused, too, still a couple of steps behind her.

"Fine," she said over her shoulder. "You asked for it."

He gave her legs another look, saw that she was on the move again, and hurried to catch her.

Chapter 18 – A Clever Crosswind

They walked toward the street in silence, sometimes bumping shoulders, and she fumbled around until she'd found his hand. A light drizzle continued to drop on them and everything else, and neither of them spoke.

She stopped them at the edge of the curb, and they both looked each way a couple of times. The stoplight at the intersection was flashing yellow for the cross traffic, and the speed limit was high and largely ignored by every vehicle racing past them.

"God," she said.

He pried his hand free of hers and leaned out, trying to look into her eyes, but she didn't turn hers from the traffic.

"God, what?"

"That's the target. It's that simple."

"Huh? What does that mean? Who's shooting at God?"

She turned to him slowly, her eyes tired.

"Have you been listening at all?"

"Yeah. Sure. All that stuff about—"

She shook her head a few times, her eyes open wider.

"It's all the same thing. It's all fucked up to get us off target."

He stared and waited, and more loudly, she said, "Guess who fucked it up."

Socrates saw beyond her that an elderly couple, dressed well and appropriately for the rainy weather, slowed then stopped, both watching Miley.

"And you haven't heard the biggest crosswind yet. Sure you want to? Are you fucking sure?"

He snapped his head around quickly and saw that a small crowd was gathering behind them, all watching as Miley, dressed to market her product, screamed at him in the early morning on the city sidewalk.

"Goddammit, Socrates, are you fucking—"

Grabbing both of her shoulders and turning her enough that they faced each other, he yelled back, "Take it easy! Jesus, Miley!"

She softened in his hold, her hunched shoulders relaxing as she took a deep breath. She nodded at him, sharing a tired smile and pointing at his face.

"Exactly. Bingo."

Still smiling, she used her pointing finger to touch him gently on the tip of his nose, and she wiggled it from side to side a few times.

Then, she looked around at all of the curious faces, holding their gazes long enough to prompt them to be on their way.

Focused again on Socrates, her short lapse of intensity depleted, she said, "The booze hasn't wasted you completely."

She spun easily out of his grasp to face the street again, smiling with her head loose and seeming to be tipping with the wind.

He said, "Huh? Bingo what? What are you—"

"Biggest goddamn crosswind ever."

"No, you can't be serious. Jesus?"

She turned to him and looked steadily into his eyes.

"Is he real? Is he what we were told? Or is it a bunch of shit that Lucifer made up?"

"Why? What for?"

She grimaced and said, "To get us off target. Think about it."

She looked away from him, eyeing the nearby people, most of whom quickly spun away and continued walking.

"What if all your devotion and worship should go to God—only to God—and Lucifer got so many of us to look away?"

She held Socrates's questioning stare and said, "That's a crosswind, Socrates. He can't get everyone to point their guns the opposite direction. So, he settled for just making them miss."

She stared at him for a moment, shaking her head and waiting for any kind of answer.

"All he needed was a clever crosswind. With that, even good people that he'd never be able to corrupt miss the target."

Silent, still, he stared back at her.

"And he's got everyone asking Jesus to save them. What if he's made up? Fake? Take a guess what God thinks of bullshit like that."

She spent another few seconds daring passersby to look her way. None accepted her offer, so she leaned in close to Socrates and whispered hoarsely.

"Jesus might be just a big fucking crosswind."

"Okay, so what if that's true? Tell the world. Set things straight."

She looked down at his right hand reaching into his pocket for the whiskey bottle, and she grabbed his wrist, stopping him.

"Dammit, stop drinking a second. You're not paying attention. What if that idea, that got burned into my skull, came from Lucifer? That idea could be aimed at getting everyone to stop giving a shit about Jesus, who might be exactly what we were told. Maybe a lot of people would stop believing in Jesus, and that would be my fault. I'd be working for the damn devil."

"Oh, right. Uh, God probably wouldn't like that."

He saw her shoulders tense, raising up, so he reached out with both hands and held her gently.

"No, he wouldn't," she said. "But if it's God's idea, he'll be pissed if I don't tell the world. He might want me to finally set the record straight. At least get people to think about it. See the fucking trap I'm in?"

"So, you can't really even kill yourself to get out of it, can you?"

"That freak won't let me anyway."

He saw that her eyes, brightening with help from the sky, had collected a soft, wet sheen, so he pulled her in close. She laid her head on his shoulder, and he rubbed slowly up and down on her arms.

He quickly found that he needed to stare back at people who had stopped long enough to gawk at the man hugging a hooker for everyone to see.

She didn't end his embrace but leaned away, eyes still wet and focused on him again.

"No, Socrates. If it's from God, killing myself would be quitting. Not doing what he wants from me. But if it's from Lucifer, all I'd be doing is committing suicide, which God probably kind of hates too. But none of it matters because that goddamn freak won't let me die anyway."

She slipped out of his loose hold to stoop down low, and his hat mostly blocked his view of her face.

He leaned close and placed a hand on her back.

"Did God give me that idea because Jesus is a scam? Or did Lucifer tell me that because Jesus is for real? How the fuck can I possibly know?"

He looked both ways, then leaned away more to try again to see her face.

"I'd say he's real, Miley. Even though I don't know."

He stood up abruptly at three loud animal yips so close behind him that he froze and didn't look. He only grimaced instead.

Miley was looking up at him, cheeks wet from the misty rain.

"Oh, really? Well, here's something for you to point your brain at."

She reached a hand up, he took it, again felt its warmth, and helped her to stand facing him.

"Liars like to play with words, right, Socrates? How about this one: fiction."

He tipped his head, squinted at her for a second, and scratched at his chin.

"Yeah, fiction means fake. It's not real. So?"

"Okay, in your head, write the word 'crucifixion.' Do you see it?"

"Yeah, but it—"

"Do you fucking see it?"

"Yeah, Miley. Yeah."

"Change the 'x' to 'ct.' Now, what do you see?"

His eyes couldn't open any wider as he stared at her, and she scoffed back at him, nodding her head.

"Holy shit," he said. "The damn devil is—"

She laughed once and said, "He's laughing his ass off because he's telling us. He put it right in our fucking faces, and we're too stupid to see it."

"Well, maybe that's just some weird coincidence or something. Since we saw that priest trying to keep you alive, that must mean—"

She grabbed his shoulders and shook him once, barely moving him.

"I don't know that that's a priest. Do you? Are you sure?"

"Damn. There's no way of knowing. How about that 'X' tattoo? Does that help?"

"Not a fucking bit. If he's with God, that might just be part of the uniform. You know, "X" for Jesus and all that. And if he's with Satan?"

"Then, um, it's just another sick devil joke."

She let her arms drop to her sides and looked down at the sidewalk.

"Crucifixion. Cross fiction. Fucking hilarious."

He leaned forward, trying to see her eyes, then something large and heavy bumped him from behind with a deep, low growl. He whipped himself around, scanning everywhere, and saw only a few pedestrians glancing at him as they passed and the last few raindrops falling into sidewalk puddles.

Past the sidewalk, above a mound of thick hedges, a furry tail flicked around, then snaked its way inside and out of sight.

Chapter 19 – I'm Finally Free

Staring at the shrubs, waiting for the tail to reappear, Socrates felt Miley take hold of both of his shoulders. She started to turn him, and he cooperated, but he kept his eyes fixed for as long as he could on the exact spot where he'd seen the beast hide itself.

He said, "Did you—," but then saw her looking intently into his eyes, her back to the street with traffic flying past them.

She took both of his hands and said, "One more time, I'm going to try to—"

She leaned and looked behind Socrates and scoffed, so he turned to see.

The priest stood several steps behind him, only the very bottom of his long coat moving with the wind and dark glasses blocking any view of his eyes. The drizzle had decreased to the extent that very little dripped off of the brim of his hat.

Socrates groaned softly and turned back around to face her.

"All I did was think about it, and it knew. Dammit, Socrates. But I just don't care anymore. I can't figure this shit out. I don't even care if it saves me or not. But it probably fucking will."

"Like every other time, huh?"

She nodded then released him, and she reached up with both hands to grab the hat that he'd given her. Still looking into his eyes, she placed it on his head.

"It looks good on you too."

Then, she began slow steps backwards, between parked cars along the curb, her eyes still locked on his.

"Wait," he said. "Don't."

"Maybe I can be quick enough. Let's find out."

"Don't, Miley. Just don't."

She shook her head and laughed, weak and tired.

"Because you'll miss me?"

"Well, yeah. Of course."

She tipped her head, and her eyes blinked slowly as she strained to give him a smile.

"'Cause you got a thing for hookers."

"No. I mean, yeah, I kind of do. But that's not why."

She paused her backwards travel, looked behind her, then back into his eyes. She struggled out another modest smile for him.

"You don't have to ask," she said. "I do care about you."

"You . . . you do?"

She nodded once, holding his gaze, then again looked past him. He turned to look and saw that the priest had moved to stand close behind him.

Socrates stared at the dark glasses for several seconds, scoffed loudly, then turned back toward Miley, who had resumed taking small, slow backwards steps toward the traffic.

She stopped before the next one would put her in danger.

He said, "I care about you too," and he noticed for the first time the color of her eyes.

Against the sea of grays and dark grays behind her, like beacons through the thickening mists, he saw her beautiful blue eyes.

She gave him a tired grin, then lost it and tipped her head.

"Really," she said, "what's the big deal with Jesus anyway?"

"Huh? What do you mean?"

An animal's shriek split the sky, and he turned quickly, leaned to look around the priest, and saw nothing.

So, he spun himself back toward Miley and stepped off of the curb. She held her palm out, convincing him to stop.

"Would you give up your life to save a stranger?" she said. "I bet you would. Lots of people do."

"Yeah, but that's not—"

After a short, sharp laugh, she said, "And you don't know that you're the actual son of God. Shit, you don't know what the hell you are. You don't even have a fucking clue if there's anything after all this. And still . . . you'd do it. You'd die for a goddamn stranger, with no one around to notice and no grand prize like offering everyone a ticket out of Hell."

Something behind Socrates howled loudly, then chattered rapidly, and he whipped himself to the left, saw nothing, then to the right, and saw that the priest had quietly moved to stand right next to him.

Socrates turned back toward her, and he and the priest watched Miley look behind her just as a car sped past.

She faced him again and said, "You'd do it for nothing at all. Just because you fucking care."

She took the next step and remained there, a gap in the line of traffic delaying any imminent threat.

Socrates turned to the priest, saw him completely immobile, and yelled to Miley.

"Miley, no! It's different this time! Come back!"

He took his first step toward her, his hands out.

"No!" she said.

He stopped his charge, but he was still reaching out to her.

"No, Socrates. Let that freak do his fucking job."

He let his arms down.

She laughed softly while shaking her head at him.

"Somehow," she said, "I'm free. I feel it. Oh, God, I'm finally free."

A loud bus horn wailed off to his left, and Socrates gave it a quick glance. It was barreling directly at her on the slick, wet pavement.

He looked back at her in time to see that she'd noticed it, too, but she turned back to him and held his gaze.

She said, "Hey, Socrates, or whatever your name is, if that freak doesn't stop me, that thing,"—she tipped her head toward the bus—"is like my own—"

She waited while the driver sounded the horn again.

"—personal—"

The horn blared and the tires began to skid.

"—goddamn—"

"Miley! Come back!"

Almost there, the driver let the horn scream out again.

Miley waited patiently for him to back off on it, then smiled and said, "—cross—"

The driver blasted his horn, the tires kept skidding and sliding roughly on the street surface, and Socrates stared into Miley's calm blue eyes, her mouth open for the rest of a word that she'd never complete.

Slicing that brief moment and taking a tiny piece for himself, Socrates imagined that her lips had formed a silent kiss for him. He took that sliver of time, with her warm kiss and the blue eyes that he already missed, and made it a memory that he'd never surrender.

And he locked it in as tight as he could, just that slice, to never allow any of what he knew would follow to become part of it.

Miley's personal crosswind delivered its own annihilating kiss, becoming a mad bull rampaging through clothes drying in the sun, tangling the finest of fabrics into the handlebars, frames, and spinning wheels lashed to its horns.

With rubber locked and squeezing aside puddles to get a grip on the pavement, the bus continued down the road, past parked cars and through traffic, until it roared out of sight beyond the nearby buildings crouching near the road.

Socrates couldn't see it anymore, but he could still hear it. The horn had stopped just before the grinding tires had brought it to a stop somewhere out of his sight.

He looked all around at people on both sides of the road rushing that way. The hands he'd pressed over his ears had no chance at blocking out the other siren approaching from the left—a police car with blue lights strobing like mad—as it sped past, too bright to be a part of that gray world.

His attempt at sprinting after her started even before he'd lowered his hands. But his first step never landed.

He felt a strong hand clamped to his coat between his shoulders, so solid and unyielding that it could have been chained to an anchor bolted to the concrete. His sudden stop jerked his head forward and if his hand hadn't still been close to his hat, he wouldn't have been able to trap it in place.

The anchor was too strong to fight, so he didn't try. He only stared at the uniform edge of bricks that began the walls of the building that hid whatever was left of the hooker that he'd met in a dark alley.

One who had shared with him an idea so menacing that she'd seen suicide as her only way out.

A woman who had told him that she cared about him.

Without him having to ask.

"Miley," he said, still staring.

He brought back that first step, stood as straight as he could, and felt the vise knotting up his coat release it.

After a raspy sigh, he said, "Her name was Miley."

Chapter 20 – Every Voice Screamed

Socrates had never closed his eyes, never averted his gaze, as he watched the road quickly return to its appearance before a bus had slaughtered Miley without anyone intervening to save her.

He had managed to block out some of the sounds of it, though, and slowly, sirens and screaming and revving engines filled what he'd forced into being a muted spectacle for him.

Despite all that noise, he heard a hungry roar call out behind him, right into his ear—a monster about to devour him. He snapped his head to the right, expecting to see the priest.

But he wasn't there, so Socrates turned himself around, his back to a road that had quieted some.

The priest was right behind him, facing him, and close enough to touch.

Dark glasses carried a few wet streaks from the light rain, which had picked up again. His cheeks were wet, too, even under the brim of his hat.

The tattooed "X" seemed to exaggerate the stillness of the figure and his total indifference to what had just happened.

"You!" Socrates said in a throttled scream. "You . . . you were supposed to—"

The priest held one finger to his lips, and Socrates never finished. He only stared in disbelief as the silent figure tipped his head and grinned.

Just a very faint grin.

Like he knew that it would be noticed no matter how small.

Socrates stared at the stingy smile and heard loud roaring from his left, then insane screeching from his right, then mad, tortured howling behind him. All of it cried out in unison as he stared only into glass too dark to disclose whether there were actual eyes behind it.

And while staring at that blackness, Socrates saw, to each side, giant, unidentifiable animals prowling past, circling around them, sometimes jumping at each other and howling at the sky.

Then, they all fell silent, and their huge, furry heads turned toward him, their eyes staring.

And they began a slow approach, all while the priest remained frozen, a grin etched beneath the "X" on his cheek.

Socrates closed his eyes, laughing and sobbing, and felt himself leaning to his left.

He groaned and straightened himself, only to begin tipping again to his left.

With his eyes still closed, he cackled continuously up into the rainfall and groaned while fighting to regain his posture.

And the animals, completely encircling him, all called to the sky with him, and he lost his voice among them—any one of those roars or screeches or howls could have been his.

When they all fell silent, so did he.

Still facing the sky, he opened his eyes and began a slow toppling to his left.

He didn't fight it.

He only screamed into the rain clouds, "We're all so goddamn lost!"

And he leaned so far that he fell and while his consciousness ebbed, he braced himself for the impending impact of his head on the concrete.

But a strong hand supported it and though it let his body drop as it would, it held his head then gently laid it down in a puddle.

When the hand pulled away roughly, it sent his hat rolling to the side, toward the circus surrounding him.

As he rested there, facedown with his cheek in a puddle, he wondered which of those beasts had tried on his hat.

He suspected that the animal would soon start hooting happily about it, bragging to the others.

But it wasn't just one of them crying out at the soggy sky.

No, they were all laughing, each with its own savage, ravenous voice.

* * *

He awoke to the sounds of animals howling and screeching and cackling as they ran circles around him, their paws splashing and their claws scraping.

The puddle was cool, not deep enough to drown him, and he stayed there with his eyes squeezed shut and hands grinding into his ears.

Their calls grew louder, and he knew that they were moving in, attacking him while he was down, eager to bite and rip and devour and—

"Stop!"

He sat up quickly, swiveling his head to look all around while he wiped one eye at a time.

No animals. Only a dusky city suffering under a light rain.

No traffic. And no pedestrians either.

His city was gray, wet, and offering no hints of ever having hosted a single life.

Something to his left caught his eye, and he spun as quickly as he could, thinking that maybe showing the beast that he saw it, that he refused to be blindsided, would stop the impending slaughter.

But nothing was there.

Just raindrops plinking into puddles.

A voice called out from behind him, a high-pitched singing, addressing him by name.

Not his real name.

He whipped around and saw a female figure in the distance.

Her legs were drawing in more than their share of the light, but her hair, dry and full and blown by the breezes, also sparkled softly like water streaming through a tattered umbrella in a dark alley.

Was it Miley? Should he run to her?

She waved an arm high over her head, and he was sure that he'd heard the word "madman."

Whose hat was she wearing? Was that his hat?

He saw two blue dots embedded in the gloom, winking on and off as she nodded the wide brim of his hat.

And as he watched, Miley's pinpoints of blue grew, blossoming out from her eyes, restoring hues and shades to every surface, and he knew that his entire city would soon be—

She laughed and stepped out of sight around a corner.

And like trash through the grate of a storm drain, the colors that she'd added to the city circled in a leisurely vortex while getting sucked around that corner, too, leaving the world gray.

The voice called him again, from another direction. Louder.

He looked and saw that she was closer.

She was so near that he saw not only her blue eyes but her smile too.

She called to him again.

She spread her arms wide, promising him a warm and safe embrace.

Inviting him to join her and the myriad colors she'd again unleashed on the city, all fanning out from her in an unstoppable, slow-motion explosion.

He started to rise but stopped suddenly when an animal growled viciously to his right.

But Socrates held himself still and refused to look away from Miley as she painted his world.

Another cried out from his left.

Several joined the ravenous chorus behind him.

His eyes closed on their own, then he heard Miley's laughter until it faded.

And he knew that she'd given up and left him to his fate.

More voices joined in, all calling to him without words as they drew near.

"Stop," he whispered to himself. "Please, dear God, make them stop."

They didn't stop.

They only got louder and closer, and he realized that all he could do was cry with what little time he had left.

Helpless, sobbing, he let himself crumple back to the pavement, and waves in the puddle against his cheek felt warm.

Something soft but powerful bumped the back of his head.

But he didn't look.

He kept his eyes locked shut.

Another bump, probably from a bear's snout, he thought, hit his lower back, nosing him around, trying to roll him over.

He fought it, desperate to not get eaten so easily.

Something big and probably with big teeth, too, began pawing at his legs, pushing them around.

Until he pulled them in close, up against his chest.

Fetal position, he remembered—that's the safest.

It was just so goddamn impossible to stay safe in such a world.

Something devious cackled in his ear, but he didn't dare let go of his knees as he renewed his tight hold.

Some animals howled. Others roared.

He'd lost count of how many were howling and roaring, pawing at him, trying to roll him over to rip him open at his softest, most palatable spots. So many wild, pungent breaths hot on his neck.

He took in a deep breath and was about to scream, then they all fell silent.

None were touching him.

He didn't dare open his eyes, and his breaths, heavy and drenched with all the rain hanging in the air, struggled in and out.

And he waited.

Until every voice screamed at once, and every paw pressed down on him at once, and he resigned himself to that first bite, that first claw.

That first warm, wet rip.

He opened his mouth to scream, and everything stopped.

All except the continuous squawking from something gigantic whose sharp claws maintained a pointy hold on his hip.

Chapter 21 – You Tell the World

He took in two strong breaths, held his hand back, ready for a futile swat at a vulture that he was sure would soon begin rending his flesh, tossing tasty morsels of it to the rest of his wake.

Already beginning a low scream, Socrates opened his eyes and dropped his hand, then stifled his unneeded scream at seeing, for less than a second, the unreadable black beads of a pigeon's eyes. A flutter of wings sent it off to his left, so he rolled that way to look.

A small flock of them were within reach, all studying him intently. He rolled to the right and saw more staring birds.

"No," he said. "No seed. Go away."

He waved his arms frantically and they all launched themselves, and he lay there another few seconds to watch airy bits of feathers float to the ground.

As the sound of their wings faded, the sounds of traffic rose. And there were people, talking as they walked past him, some laughing at the man lying in a puddle.

He sat up, and rubbed the puddle water off of his face, and looked around at everything just the way he'd left it.

With Miley still gone. No blue anywhere.

But the priest was still there.

A hand was extended to him, one coated in tattooed patterns and symbols.

Socrates grabbed his hat from the sidewalk near him, then accepted the help and was lifted easily to stand and face the figure.

Without expression, the priest said, "Your beasts left you here."

"Dammit. You let her die? Before she could tell the world?"

The priest smirked, one so slight that Socrates might not have seen it but that he was staring so fixedly at that face.

He glared at the figure, then turned to run again toward Miley or whatever of her might still be found.

But the priest's grip on his arm stopped him dead—anchored again. Before trying to free himself or turning to scream at the man, he heard his calm voice.

"She won't be coming back."

He jerked his arm free and turned to face him.

"Why did she say that she was free? She's free because she's dead?"

He watched the dark glasses shift slowly from side to side.

"She's gone because she became free."

"What? What the hell does that mean?"

Socrates glanced down to see one finger on a raised tattooed hand pointing at him.

"It's only you now. You tell the world."

"Oh, fuck," he said, glancing up again, into the rain.

"Fuck," he said, again staring at the dark lenses. "Which side are you on? Dammit, come on already."

Socrates was watching for a grin or a grimace or even a smirk. He saw nothing.

"No," said the priest. "Too easy. It must be your choice."

"What? Oh, fucking free will? That's a real thing?"

The priest shrugged and said, "Rules."

He was still staring at the priest, who'd only looked back at him silently, when he felt a bulky animal, soft like a rug, drag across his back. He turned as quickly as he could but saw only a thick, fuzzy tail jiggling into the same line of shrubs.

"Jesus. What the hell? Did you—"

He turned back toward the priest, but he'd left without a sound.

Socrates gave the street another long study and could see no sign that anything disastrous with a bus had happened.

He quietly watched a slender river of rainwater, flowing along the curb and carrying discarded things somewhere out of sight.

After prying his eyes from the gutter, he gazed at the building's brick corner to his right.

A long moment passed, then he turned away from the bustling street, adjusted his collar, and began the walk home.

* * *

The rain had increased, as had the foot traffic all around him in both directions, and Socrates kept himself focused on just making it home.

Not on Miley and what had happened to her.

Not on what she'd told him—the biggest crosswind.

Not on a freak priest pointing at him, saying he was now the one.

But he couldn't ignore the feeling that there were beasts, big and hungry, following closely behind him.

"I don't know what you all want from me," he said over his shoulder.

He felt sure that one of them had swiped its long claws, just missing ripping open his back.

"I don't know why you can't just leave me alone already!"

He heard the low growling, the muffled roars, a laughing cackle, and he began a sprint, dodging people until the animal cries behind him had faded and all he could hear was the rain and the traffic and his shoes splashing and pounding the pavement.

* * *

With his building in sight, still obscured by sheets of falling rain and clouds of mist, he checked again and confirmed that no beasts had been able to keep up.

So, he slowed to a walk, eyes straight ahead and hands in his pockets.

Rain cascaded off of the brim of his hat.

Seconds later, he stopped abruptly and drew in a deep breath.

He turned quickly and saw the priest a dozen steps behind him, motionless.

Just standing there and studying him.

"Dammit," he said to himself.

Then, he lunged to his right, straight toward traffic.

And he felt that he must have somehow moved in slow motion, because the priest moved more quickly than any living thing could.

He stopped between Socrates and the road, and Socrates slid to a quick stop. Then, the priest calmly turned toward him.

No expression.

Nothing to say.

His eyes still on the silent priest, Socrates started slow steps toward the doorway that he knew would take him into a bright, colorful world, and he mumbled to himself but loud enough that the priest could hear it too.

"You son of a bitch. You should have saved her."

The priest's dark glasses stared back, and he remained silent.

"You should have fucking saved her."

Socrates leveled his hat brim and fought the urge to look back at the priest again as he resumed his hurried final steps to the door.

Chapter 22 – Write a Special Story

He came to a quick stop, then swung open the heavy glass door to his building and stepped through, where he paused just inside the lobby to drag a few drops of water off of the sleeves of his coat.

Before looking toward the burgundy couch, his favorite piece of furniture in the spacious room, maybe everywhere, he realized, he looked up at all of the twinkling lights hanging from the ceiling. Each one seemed like a tiny sun compared to the unbroken gray ceiling outside.

He scanned all around, taking in all of the colors and trying to find any areas of shadows. If they were there, they'd hidden themselves well.

Then, he let himself check the couch and with the anticipation of who he hoped to see there, he almost forgot the weight that he'd taken upon his back, the burden that had broken Miley.

But he didn't try to forgot that his friend, Miley, was gone.

Wendy was there, and Rae Cat was beside her.

Wendy still wore her light jeans but had put on a yellow t-shirt instead of her pink sweatshirt.

Rae still wore her black coat.

"Can't beat a little black coat," he said softly to himself.

Wendy waved and smiled, but Rae did neither of those things.

He gave a quick wave back to her, then took the short walk and soon stood near, looking down on the young girl and her cat.

"Hi, Mr. Lewis. Did you feed the birds?"

He gazed at her, unable to speak for a long moment, even though he knew that his mouth was making an attempt.

"I, uh . . . I'm so happy to see you, Wendy. Don't ever go away, okay?"

"I won't. I'm not allowed."

"That's right. You're not. Rae Cat too, alright?"

"We won't. What about the birds, Mr. Lewis? Did you feed them already?"

He coughed and said, "I, um, yeah. I got an early start today."

No longer smiling, Wendy nodded while she spoke.

"That's a good story."

Socrates stared at the child, his mouth still open, then he looked at the cat. The cat looked back.

"No, really, Wendy. Sure, it was earlier than usual, but the birds—"

Wendy gave him an amused laugh and shook her head.

"It's a good story that people feed birds. They're always hungry. I was and ate a lot of cereal today."

"Oh, right. Yeah, that sure is a good story. I get it. A story about feeding birds."

"Will you write about that today?"

He stared at the girl then up at the ceiling, barely noticing the tiny suns fastened to chains and keeping them hanging straight.

"Write about it?"

He looked back down at her, and she smiled and nodded.

"Wendy, you're a genius! You too, Rae. Yes, I'm going to write a very special story as soon as I can."

He took a moment to smile at the girl, whose eyebrows were kept high up. Then, he studied the cat, who showed clearly that she didn't care about any of it.

"I know exactly what to do!"

Socrates gave Wendy one more enthusiastic smile, then sped toward the stairs and sprinted all the way up, never counting or tallying areas of pesky purple circles as they zoomed past beneath his stomping shoes.

Wendy leaned over toward her cat and said, "We're geniuses, Rae!"

Chapter 23 – On Your Head, Mara

He skipped over the red, orange, and yellow objects littering the hallway and rushed to get inside his apartment. With the door shut behind him, he paused and looked around.

"There's more light in here? How?"

Still staring at his place, seeing more colors than the last time he'd been there, he reached behind without looking and found that the light switch was off.

"Huh. Weird. Even without that."

He peeled off his coat and dumped it on a kitchen chair, then tossed his hat somewhere near, but it fell to the floor. He left it there and rushed into his bedroom.

Before taking the few extra steps needed to slam shut the window, he stopped to check his degree of leaning with the string and the ring.

He confirmed that he was leaning to the left but not by much. He laughed at the sight of it, then brushed at his left shoulder a few times.

"Whichever one of you is there, you're the heavy one, huh?"

Still smiling, his eyes were drawn to the whiskey bottle, which he picked up and poured. He let it go, trading it for the glass, which he held up for a toast to himself.

"Heavy, light, good, evil. How the hell can anyone know?"

He took a generous swig, then held it out all the way to his right. He saw the mirror man leaning to the right, so he drew back the glass a little at a time until he was straight.

"And who cares? I know what to do. Wendy told me. Or maybe it was that Rae Cat of hers. Either way, I know now. I'll just—"

He stopped himself and turned to give the open window above his nightstand a serious study for a moment, then he walked to it and leaned to get a good look outside.

Tipping his head a few times and turning to listen, he heard only the light rainfall and distant sounds of traffic.

"Where are all you hungry animals, huh?" he called to the outside. "You're back in the goddamn jungle where you always belonged."

Laughing, he looked around at the pleasant colors, even of the brick buildings crowding in close across the alley.

Then, he slammed it shut.

*   *   *

With a glass half full of whiskey in his hand, Socrates hummed softly and began the short hike out of his bedroom, but he came to an abrupt stop and looked over at the dresser.

A few steps later, he got his grip around the bottle's neck and picked it up to eye level, swirling it around.

"Running low. Still, it's enough to help restart that writing career of mine. And that would be . . . good. She even said so."

With the bottle and glass, he resumed his walk toward the kitchen, saying to himself, almost laughing about it, "Jesus, I really was going to stop talking to myself. Well, hell, maybe I should at least change the name I always use."

He kicked the chair back and sat, facing the typewriter and its blank canvas rolled snugly around the platen and the ribbon poised to print out the first letter of his first work in months.

Before setting the bottle down, he topped off his glass, then pinched the ribbon, smiling at the ink stains on his fingers.

"Jesus, that ink has been more patient than me."

After wiping most of it off on his pant leg, he began typing furiously, slamming the carriage return lever hard enough to rotate the entire typewriter a small amount each time. Every couple of sentences, he stopped to set it straight.

And to take a drink.

When one hand snapped each crowded sheet up and out, the other was already groping for the next to take its place.

Finally, done with the last page, he located his finger above the "period" key, then looked again at the nearly completed piece, which needed only that last bit of punctuation.

With a satisfied snort, he tapped it, saw it appear neatly in the proper location, and pulled his hands away.

Holding the glass in his right hand, he yanked the filled sheet up and out and held it there to study. His proofreading never paused as he raised the glass and sipped, and he finished both tasks at the same time.

"Crosswinds. You even wrote the damn title, Miley," he said, and gave his statement its own ending punctuation by dinging the empty glass on the table.

"It'll be on your head, Mara. I'm not testing that freak priest by waltzing into traffic."

Giving all of the sheets another scan, he looked aside only enough to aim the bottle for a refill, then he set it down and barely noticed that he was sliding it back and forth, using spilled birdseed like tiny ball bearings.

"And you damn well better decide to tell the world and publish this in that stupid mag of yours. After that, shit, go jump off a bridge. I won't stop you. Neither will that tattooed bastard out there."

With the last page of the manuscript still hanging from his left hand, he held the whiskey glass up for a toast.

"Miley was right—that was a big crosswind. Her last."

He held the glass to his lips and hesitated.

"I miss you, Miley."

Chapter 24 – Just Mailing a Letter

Socrates stood beside his cluttered kitchen table and finished what was left in his glass, then set it down. He quickly slipped on his coat, dropped the hat in place, then stopped to jam his hands into the pockets and wiggle them around.

Across the table, the two plastic seed containers waited, pressed together. He leaned forward enough to see that their levels didn't match—the one on the left was noticeably higher.

"Yep. One's heavier."

He straightened up and pointed at both of them.

"Just like my shoulders, huh? Which one of you is good, and which one is evil?"

He laughed at his own joke, then walked to the door, where he switched off the lights. And he paused there, looking all around.

It was much brighter than he would have expected.

"Huh."

He pulled the door shut behind him and didn't check the lock. But he did take a second to look all along the hallway carpet's chaotic assortment of red, orange, and yellow bits and pieces that seemed alive and swimming around under light from a ceiling full of suns hanging from chains.

He muffled his next laugh, suspecting that a young girl and her cat, mainly her cat, would hear it, then he aimed for the stairs with a sealed envelope in one hand. There, he looked down at a bumpy slide coated with pale purple circles, all mingling and dancing around on the surface of a dark, murky purple sea.

Two steps at a time, he stepped over most of them, and he'd reached the bottom before he let himself look for the burgundy couch.

Where Wendy always sat.

With Rae Cat.

They were there. They hadn't gone away, and the girl had already begun to smile. But the cat only yawned once and stared.

Socrates waved and hurried toward the couch, his arms swinging and the envelope in his hand obvious.

"Hi, Wendy. Hello, Rae Cat."

"Hi, Mr. Lewis. Time to feed the birds again?"

He stopped to return the cat's indifferent stare before turning back to Wendy and flashing the envelope for her to see.

"Not this time, Wendy. Just mailing a letter."

She giggled and began petting the cat with her left hand while her right still held closed a stuffed brown paper bag on the couch beside her. She let go of it to point at the letter Socrates had just typed for Mara.

"It's full of bird seed!"

He held it out, gave it a glance, and laughed heartily.

"Oh, Wendy, no. I'll deliver that personally later. Again. They always want more."

The girl shook her head while observing the thin envelope, then turned her eyes toward Socrates again.

"I don't think I'd like to just eat seeds."

"No, of course not. What do you suppose you'd like the least about it?"

She scrunched up her face, looked around, then found a smile and looked back up at him.

"It's all the same color. I like my cereal—it's all kinds of colors."

"Huh. You're right."

Nodding, he turned to begin his walk toward the door, still smiling at Wendy.

"That Rae Cat is kind of just one color, though."

She looked down at the black cat who looked nowhere else but at Socrates. Wendy wiggled the cat's ears around and studied her closely, her face serious.

"Her eyes, Mr. Lewis. Her eyes are green. That's all the color she needs."

Socrates had his hand on the door and was about to swing it open. But he held himself still and looked first at Rae, then Wendy.

"Blue eyes are good, too, Wendy. I . . . like blue eyes."

He paused to look through the glass, not at his reflection, and saw a world brimming with colors and light, even though the rain hadn't diminished and the skies still hid the city under a quilt of spongy clouds.

Chapter 25 – Either Heaven or Hell

"The city's lovely today," he said to a neighbor passing him to get into the building.

She stopped, glanced at the rain hitting the street, then stared at him for just a second with a distinct squint.

"It's all yours," she said, and Socrates stepped aside for her.

Sheets of rain, sweeping along parallel to the street, caused countless tiny splashes in puddles everywhere, and he listened to it drumming softly on the canopy, the strands of its fringed edges dripping steadily.

He adjusted his collar, leveled out the brim of his hat, then tucked the envelope inside his coat. He'd taken only a few steps out into the rain, traveling to his left—not to the park to feed the birds, just to the nearest mailbox—when he caught his breath and swiveled his head to look toward the street.

And he scoffed at his own involuntary reaction. Not fight and not flight. He knew that neither of those would do any good. Instead, he noticed that he'd pressed his back firmly against the wet brick wall.

And he was certain that that wouldn't do any good either.

The priest was there, on the very edge of the curb and ignoring Socrates. Facing the direction of his travel.

He still wore his long, dark coat, a dark, wide-brimmed hat, and dark glasses unneeded on a rainy day.

Even from that distance, Socrates could see a splotch on his cheek. And he knew what it was.

"That's not a goddamn 'CT.'"

Not caring about whatever wear and tear or damage might be inflicted on the back of his coat, he shuffled one step to his left, feeling the cloth drag across the rough surface.

The priest also took one step.

He tried another step.

So did the priest.

"Who are you? Who sent you?"

The priest showed no reaction, and the light rain continued to drip off of the brim of his hat in unchanging locations from him holding so still. He could have been a statue.

Socrates scoffed and said, "Well, the hell with this, then."

He lunged two quick steps toward the street, and the priest instantly turned toward him, crouching slightly and with his arms out to his sides.

Socrates froze, and so did the priest.

After a long moment of staring into the blank, dark lenses hiding the priest's eyes, if he had any, Socrates retreated until he'd again plastered his back onto the brick wall.

Only then did the priest turn to face their shared travel direction, and he waited, again behaving like a statue.

Socrates scoffed loudly and resumed his journey to mail the letter to Mara, occasionally stopping to bump his left shoulder into the wall to straighten himself up.

*　*　*

Many steps later, interspersed with glances, some furtive and others overt, in the direction of his silent companion, Socrates had reached the mailbox. It occupied a spot near the curb, as the priest continued to do, too, but several steps distant.

He grabbed the handle on the chute door and stopped, looking into the face obscured by dark glasses and advertising his allegiance to . . . someone. With a large "X" on his cheek.

121

"I get it," Socrates said to him above the nearby clatter of traffic. "What Miley was saying. Who is it that wants that idea out in the world? Who's paying your salary, huh?"

The priest continued to stare or at least point his glasses toward Socrates, who sighed and looked down at the mailbox handle.

"Somebody wants me alive. If I dump this bullshit on Mara, then you can go spook the hell out of her instead. How's that sound? I'm free of it, then, right?"

He looked up and scoffed at the priest's lack of response.

"Dammit. You're just following orders, huh?"

The priest remained silent and motionless, so Socrates again looked at the mailbox and the letter to Mara.

"Goddamn it, I thought I knew what to do. But I don't."

He quickly looked out over the busy street when he heard a rough grunt behind him, low, near the sidewalk surface.

He didn't try to see whatever beast had crept up behind him.

A howl, louder than the grunt, held its tone, rising and falling, then trailing away to allow the traffic to dominate again.

Still gazing out at the row of tall brick structures looming across the street, Socrates noticed that their rusty color was dimming, as if more effective clouds had been summoned. The kind that could easily blend every known color into a gray mush.

The city around him darkened, welcoming a pervasive blandness that clung to every surface, every vehicle, and every passerby, none of them aware of the battle being waged between a lone man with an envelope—and an idea—and an agent from either Heaven or Hell.

He looked down at the metal box that had been a pleasant shade of blue just moments earlier, but it, too, had succumbed to the creeping death of color surrounding it.

"Yeah, Mara's a pain in the ass sometimes. Maybe not as much as you, you son of a bitch. But she doesn't deserve this."

He let go of the handle and turned enough to stare comfortably at the silent priest, still several steps away and standing near the curb.

Before he could express any more disgust, Socrates got bumped from behind by something large enough to move him easily, and it grunted softly, then bumped him again.

Not taking his eyes off of the priest, Socrates said, "One of your friends?"

The priest offered no comment.

"An angel buddy? No. No, that was some kind of a beast."

He had to keep watching him, but he knew that he wouldn't get an answer.

Looking down, speaking only for his own benefit, Socrates said, "I don't know what the fuck to do."

He looked up and said, "Hey, why don't you just tell the world?"

The priest didn't even tip his head. The light rain continued to drip off of his hat brim.

"I didn't think so. Bastard. Even if you're an angel, you're a bastard. I mean, really. What the fuck . . ."

He began a solemn hike back to his building, Miley's fateful idea, carefully typed out and addressed to Mara, safe from the rain inside his coat.

Only a few times did he look toward the road, each time to see the priest matching his steps, stopping when he stopped and facing straight ahead.

With a silent shadow character walking along with him through a drab and dingy city, Socrates plodded and sometimes splashed through the incessant rain.

Chapter 26 – Wendy, You're a Genius

The door fought to stay closed from the wind leaning against it, but Socrates pried it open enough to slip inside. With his back to it, he let the gusts close it but not slam it as he brushed water off of his sleeves.

A meager smile appeared when he looked up at the hanging lights, bright like tiny suns. He gave the walls, all blues and greens, and artwork, replete with every color imaginable, a quick study, then turned his eyes toward the burgundy couch.

He'd hoped that he could manage a more genuine smile at seeing Wendy there, but it resisted his best efforts to dig it up and display it. A forced one would have to do.

Still, he began a walk that would take him near her but was also almost a direct route to the stairs.

"Hi, Wendy. It's a good day to stay dry inside."

He kept walking, giving her only quick glances along the way.

"Hi, Mr. Lewis. Did you mail your letter?"

He'd already passed her, and he kept his back to her when he stopped to answer.

"No. I, um, can't. I couldn't."

He resumed his hike, already getting his eyes tangled up with the troublesome purple patterns of the stair runners.

"You can still keep feeding the birds."

He nodded, still looking away and hoping that she'd seen it, then lifted his leg for the first step on the first rectangular corral of light purple dots.

Wendy sat with Rae Cat and watched Socrates until he'd traveled too far for anyone in the lobby to see.

*   *   *

In the quiet lobby, on a burgundy couch, an eight-year-old girl named Wendy sat with a black cat that she'd named Rae beside her. The girl was humming softly, monitoring the cat's activity and petting her gently, both of them bathed in bright light.

They both looked up at the sound of heavy footfalls rushing down the steps, and they saw Socrates, still wearing his coat and holding his hat in place, stomping as quickly as he could to the bottom.

He never slowed. His first step on the clean tile floor was the beginning of a sprint to traverse the short distance, and he stood looking down on girl and cat, his breaths heavy from the exertion.

He waged an awkward battle with himself, staring only at the cat, pointing at her and saying, "She . . . your cat . . ."

Rae Cat was eating her food from two bowls. Both were filled with brownish chunks. Except that one bowl's chunks had some tempting orange highlights.

He wiped a hand roughly all over his face, locked his stare on Wendy, and said, "Rae Cat is eating from two bowls, Wendy?"

Wendy nodded, looking up at him, and said, "She has two foods now."

She held up two fingers for a second, then wiggled them for another second.

"Mom bought another kind. Rae can't decide."

He looked back at the cat, and they both listened to her bumping the pieces along the ceramic as she nosed them around.

"So, you just give her two bowls, then?"

Wendy grinned at him, shrugged once, and continued watching her cat.

"So," said Socrates, "she eats half from one bowl and half from the other?"

Wendy had started giggling before she even looked up at him.

"No, Mr. Lewis! She eats the same amount like before—from each bowl!"

Socrates watched and listened for a moment and so did Wendy.

"How?"

The girl leaned toward Socrates, looked each way, then back up at him, and whispered, "I think she started eating twice as much! She's twice as hungry now!"

While looking from the cat to the girl and back to the cat, Socrates's smile took hold and grew. A genuine smile.

"Wendy, you're a genius!"

"I am?"

"Yes! And your cat! You and Rae together!"

Socrates made a dash toward the exit, and Wendy watched him until he'd fled out of the building. Then, she leaned toward the black cat with green eyes, who had paused to watch his rapid departure too.

"We still don't know what a genius is, Rae."

The cat resumed her meals, and Wendy resumed petting her softly.

Then, she giggled and said, "Oh, maybe you do."

Chapter 27 – We Can Only Believe

Outside, Socrates didn't linger beneath the soaked fabric roof. He stowed the envelope safely inside his coat and rushed out to his left, even though the priest was still near the curb, watching through dark glasses.

They both hurried along, the priest easily keeping up, until Socrates had reached the mailbox. He looked down at it to grab the chute handle, and he saw how blue the metal had been painted.

The priest had retaken his prior position, and he resumed his motionless study of Socrates and his letter.

"I figured it out," he said to the masklike face. "I know the answer, and I'll tell Mara and everyone else."

He gave the priest a moment to at least acknowledge that he'd spoken, but the figure remained silent. So, Socrates laughed once at the sky, then again looked in his direction.

"Double. Just double it."

No reaction.

"Maybe it's a loophole, but it should work. Even if Jesus is fake, give him all that you can. Everything in your heart."

Socrates grinned at the sight of the priest tipping his head but nothing more—the first reaction from him in a long while.

"Don't stop doing that. Just give the same amount to God too. You double it. You just have to find some way to double all of it."

The priest straightened up but said nothing, and there was no change in his blank look. Socrates scoffed at him, pulled open the mailbox door, and tossed the envelope inside.

He gazed at the solemn figure as he noisily clanged it shut.

"Acceptable? It should be. I'll tell Mara and together, we'll tell everyone else. That's the end of that fucking crosswind."

The priest didn't appear to have heard any of it.

"No matter who you work for," he said, pointing. "God isn't getting left out, and he should be happy, right? Or at least think we're being reasonable? When we double it, we have it all covered pretty damn well."

The priest offered a very faint grin, then raised one hand to point past Socrates.

He turned to look and saw the traffic on the cross street, unremarkable and moving steadily through the early morning rain.

At the sound of a low rumble, he looked to his left and saw a bus approaching, still far from them.

Still watching it, he felt a bump and turned just enough to see that the priest had relocated to stand beside him, and he'd brushed their shoulders together. He turned his head more and watched as the priest leaned forward, pointing the dark glasses toward the bus.

"No," said Socrates, putting a long step between them. "No way. I'm not killing myself now."

The priest showed no response.

"Hey, wait a minute. You didn't care about Miley killing herself. And now, you're telling me to kill myself?"

The priest was silent, his eyes, if he had any, pointed toward their left.

"No one on God's team would do that. You're with the fucking devil. Admit it."

The priest stayed quiet but took a step forward, straightened himself up, and continued pointing his expressionless face toward the bus.

"And that means that Jesus is the real deal. Everything about him. You losers might have played with prayers and words and the letter 'X' and things, but not with him. He's for real."

He waited for a response, got none, then scoffed at the silent figure.

"I'm not telling anyone about Miley's idea, and neither is Mara. I'll make sure of that. I'll get that fucking letter back somehow if I have to wrestle the damn mailman."

The priest turned his head toward Socrates and said, "Rules," then he tipped his hat's wide brim toward the oncoming bus.

Socrates snapped his head toward the bus, then back to the priest.

"What? Rules about what? You mean, about suicide?"

The quiet priest didn't answer, and he started a slow walk out into the street.

"So, you had to let Miley choose because you didn't need her anymore? That's what the goddamn free will rules say? You really are on God's team?"

The priest had reached the middle of the bus's lane, and he turned to face it.

"Now, you? You're killing yourself too?"

At getting no reaction, Socrates scoffed and said, "Fine. I get it. We solved that fucking crosswind, so your work here is done. That's how you send yourself back to Hell."

The priest didn't even look toward Socrates, and the bus, approaching rapidly, hadn't started working its horn.

"Who cares? Go. I think doubling is a good plan. Try being less of a bastard and at least tell me if you agree."

He heard the engine getting louder, and he watched as the priest turned only his head toward him. Then, he grinned.

Then, he clapped his hands together three times slowly.

"What the hell does that mean?"

The bus's horn was still silent, but its engine was screaming, and the priest was still grinning at Socrates as he stood directly in its path.

"No, wait! Not yet! Just fucking wait!"

The bus raced past, its horn never used, and at the moment that it appeared to strike the priest, there was a small explosion of water, like it had only hit a water-filled pothole.

It had never slowed. Its horn had nothing to say.

And Socrates kept staring at the place where there had been an odd, tattooed priest only a second earlier.

He laughed, almost hysterically, as he kept staring, drawing odd looks from people around him.

"Were you clapping because God liked that plan? You work for him?"

He looked each way along the crowded street, traffic moving no differently than before.

But people had stopped to stare at him.

Socrates's smile weakened then died.

"Or did you clap because Satan will get his way? Lucifer sent you? The Old Serpent?"

There was no answer, and he saw only the grayness of a city going about its usual business.

Except for the growing crowd of curious faces.

He was still staring, with no trace of a smile, when something large and furry bumped him from behind, almost lifting him off of the sidewalk.

Staring straight ahead still, with eyes about to roll out onto the pavement, he fought for every deep breath that he took.

A different breath, hot on his neck, led to the certainty that his head would soon be removed by powerful jaws. The fangs were ready, their sharp points about to break skin. He felt them.

Many human eyes were looking his way. Or maybe at the beast about to devour him. Maybe the entire spectacle.

His heart raced and threatened to notch it up even more.

He let a deep sigh escape with a pained rattle.

Feeling his heart pounding, he said, "Oh, God, I don't even care anymore. Miley said she cared about me. Let them eat me."

Then, his heart began to slow.

He blinked a few times, and his breaths began to settle.

"Is that you, Rae Cat?"

He laughed once.

"You've grown, huh? Well, of course. You're eating twice as much. Oh yeah, and your green eyes are beautiful too."

Without looking, he reached behind him, found the beast's solid flank, thick with coarse fur, and patted it a few times. He laughed again when he felt the unseen animal release his neck, rest its massive, shaggy head against his back, and keep it there.

Still tapping its side lightly, Socrates saw colors and cheerful light returning to his city.

Not growing out of two unforgettable blue eyes.

Just taking root everywhere all at once, like seeds of it had rained down from an array of suspended suns.

He let out a deep sigh, then spoke calmly.

"Alright. Enough already. There's no goddamn way I'll ever figure this out, is there?"

The animal was still up against him, and Socrates felt it bouncing into his back as it let out a few choppy roars.

"No," he said, laughing himself, "there just isn't any way to know. Not anything."

He gave the beast one final, warm rub, then pulled his hand back.

"I think maybe we're finally done, huh?"

He felt the beast bump his back just once, then it retreated without a sound.

Socrates ignored the onlookers and began the short walk back toward his apartment building. Breaks in the cloud cover allowed a few unfamiliar slivers of sunlight to parade all around him on the wet concrete, sending sparkles dancing across the puddles each time the last of the raindrops fell.

He stopped, leaned far to his right, then far to his left, then returned to straight up.

"We can't know."

Walking again, standing as straight up as a string hanging on a mirror with an engagement ring available for a far better use, he said, "We can only believe."

132

Next for Socrates Lewis

Crossovers – Socrates Lewis Stories Book Two

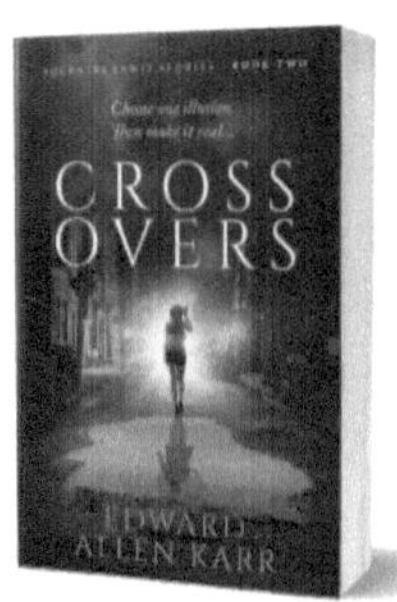

With a heavy heart from losing a friend in a tragedy that he couldn't prevent, Socrates Lewis still finds comfort in feeding the birds and his playful conversations with Wendy and her cat, Rae Cat. The whiskey helps too.

But his life gets a fresh upheaval when someone new invites herself to his bird-feeding ritual. Or is she from his very recent past? He might never solve that mystery. He might even like the not-knowing part of it, true to his adopted name.

With Aspin, he retraces almost every experience he had with Miley in that single, rainy night. Everything she says and does maneuvers him into a near-death realization, something that he knew in his heart but had never said.

He needed to say it. And she'd risk killing him to hear it.

About the Author

Edward Allen Karr was born, raised, and continues to reside in Ohio, USA. His adult life has followed a meandering path, ranging from working an automotive assembly line to designing space flight hardware. And through all of it, he's seen that life is a captivating and ultimately unexplainable endeavor. His writing seeks to add a splash of wonder to a world already awash in it.

For more about Edward Allen Karr and his writing, visit
LakesideLetters.com

* * *